PHARAOH

And

The King

Viswanath Venkat Dasari

NOTION PRESS

NOTION PRESS

India. Singapore. Malaysia.

PHARAOH And The King
By Viswanath Venkat Dasari (Vis Dasari)

1st Edition: November 2011
2nd Edition: May 2022 (Revised)

*Dedicated to the people who espouse
the path of righteousness.*

Also By Vis Dasari

THE VICTORIAN
Fable Of A Spy Who Conquered Himself

Nuggets of Knowledge
A Collection Of Snippets on Ancient India

Acknowledgments

(For This Edition)

- To the great God within me that made me to be.
- My mother Satya (Bobby); Father Radhakrishna, Younger sister Saija, for making me knowledgeable on the divine world and for giving a lot of moral support...
- My Master Teacher Ramtha, My spiritual Sibling Jz Knight, and Ascended Masters Sri Krishna and Sai Baba of Shirdi, for their guidance that gave me willpower.

Prologue

Pharaoh and the King, is the glory of a man who achieved the greater altitudes by saving the world from the hands of iniquity, that takes you back in time of Ancient civilizations, a time of Mystery, Adventure, Menace, righteousness, and to the world of supernatural truths, that reveals the occults beyond...

Angelina Adams
13/9/2011
Forster, NSW, Australia.

1

Facing destiny

25th July, 1999, the monsoon reached its peak, drenching everything in sight. The rain eventually subsided in the Himalayas, leaving the snow-capped peaks towering over a military camp near the Indo-Pak border. Tents sagged under the weight of water, and military trucks glistened with moisture from the relentless downpour. The season brought gentle breezes and vibrant wildflowers, painting the camp in shades of green.

"I thought this would be the end of the conflict that's dragged on for 30 days… but I was wrong. I couldn't see this disaster coming," muttered Lt. Colonel Raju, the lone figure standing on the muddy plateau's edge. At 34, he cut a striking figure—tall, with jet-black hair, a trimmed mustache, a hint of a beard, and piercing brown eyes. His soaked army uniform clung to him, a testament to the storm he'd endured.

He didn't believe in god, but he had faith in humanity and the tangible world. His peers revered him as a living embodiment of justice, a man whose sole mission was to shield his nation. His name was Raju.

Just steps away, a Brigadier lay lifeless on the sodden ground, felled by a single bullet. Raju stared at the body, lost in thought, when a harsh voice shattered the silence behind him. "Raajuuu, you traitor! You killed our Brigadier?!"

He turned around to find himself surrounded by his own comrades, their weapons aimed at him. A Colonel stepped forward, fury in his eyes. "Shoot him!" he bellowed, shoving Raju toward the armed troop. Confusion gripped Raju as he dropped to his knees, his face a mask of emptiness. Yet, in his brown eyes, a storm of rage brewed as he faced the barrels of his teammates' guns, poised to fire.

* * *

The citizens of Delhi poured out of their homes in the early morning, their hearts alight with joy as the radio crackled with news of victory in the war. Clutching the tricolor flag, they surged through the main streets, shouting "Jai Hind!" in unison. For a fleeting moment, the burdens of the past—the tension, the hardship, the endless worry—melted away. Families of the soldiers swelled with pride for their loved ones who had secured this triumph, and wives awaited their husbands' return, eager to share in the celebration. Among them was Sunehri, who had spent a sleepless night, her eyes fixed on the news, desperate for any word of her husband, Raju, from whom she'd heard nothing.

As dawn broke, newspapers landed on doorsteps, brimming with detailed accounts of the conflict, arriving even before the soldiers themselves. A dog darted from the lawn, snatching the paper in its jaws and trotting to the door, tail wagging furiously. Sunehri, standing there, took it from her loyal pet. "Good girl," she murmured, ruffling the dog's fur, before turning her attention to the front page. Bold headlines and vivid photographs of the war dominated the layout. Her eyes skimmed the subheadings:

"THE HEROES BEHIND THE SUCCESS OF OPERATION VIJAY --- Page 2"

"LIST OF SOLDIERS WHO SACRIFICED THEIR LIVES --- Page 3"

She flipped to the third page, but before she could read, her five-year-old son, Vivék, bounded toward her, calling, "Mã! When will Daddy come home?" Startled, Sunehri turned to him, the newspaper slipping from her grasp as a gust of wind tore through, scattering the pages across the floor. Vivék scooped one up and stared at it, his small face lighting up with innocent wonder. "Daddy is home! Daddy is home… with Grandpa!" he chirped, pointing at photographs of Raju and Mukhesh. "Can you let them out of the page, Mã?"

Sunehri's heart sank as realization dawned. She lunged forward, snatching the page from his hands, and scanned the article with growing dread:

TRAITOR SHOT FOR KILLING THE BRIGADIER

Kargil, 26th July

Amid the army's heroic sacrifices, a dark incident has cast a shadow over the victory. Just a day before the triumph, Brigadier Mukhesh Ghosh was found dead in his tent under suspicious circumstances. Colonel Vishãl Chowdary, an eyewitness, claimed, "Lieutenant Colonel Dharmaraju killed the brigadier to protect a terrorist. We had no choice but to shoot him on the spot. He was a traitor, leaking secrets to the enemy." Yet, fellow officers dispute this, insisting, "Raju would never murder his own godfather, Mukhesh. This is a lie." Questions linger: Why did Colonel Vishãl take lethal action rather than deliver Raju to a court? The truth remains shrouded in mystery. The government has ordered the army to recover their bodies and transport them to Delhi...

Sunehri stood frozen, her blue eyes brimming with tears, her pulse racing. She fought to hold herself together in front of Vivék. "Where's Dad? Let him out of the paper!" he demanded again. Without a word, she rushed inside, hiding the page where he couldn't find it. Though it was a national holiday, she dressed him for school anyway, needing a moment to breathe. Then, she took him to Mrs. Ganga Goswamy's house, their kind neighbor—a war widow of 68 who treated Raju and Sunehri like family, living with her married daughter and grandson.

"Is everything alright, dear?" Mrs. Goswamy asked, her voice gentle. Sunehri's face betrayed her grief, though she tried to mask it. She said nothing, her silence speaking volumes. After sending Vivék to play with Mrs. Goswamy's grandson, Vijju, she shared the devastating news. "I can't believe it," Mrs. Goswamy gasped. "A son wouldn't harm his father! We should demand a tribunal!"

Sunehri bowed her head, tears streaming down her cheeks like glistening pearls. "No, Ma," she whispered, her voice quaking. "I can't bear this… I don't want to live without him. Let me end it."

Mrs. Goswamy placed a tender hand under Sunehri's chin, lifting her gaze. "You mustn't, dear," she said firmly. "You have a duty to raise your son into a good man. Loving Raju doesn't mean abandoning his child. Be strong. When I lost my husband in the war thirty-seven years ago, I could've given up—but then I wouldn't have my daughter, my son-in-law, my grandson. Don't dwell on the past or the future. Live now."

Her words pierced through Sunehri's despair, anchoring her shattered heart. "I will," she said, resolve flickering in her voice. Just then, a car horn blared outside, and she turned toward the door, her breath catching in her throat.

A sleek black Mercedes-Benz rolled to a stop in front of the porch. Sunehri's breath caught as a striking figure emerged—a tall, handsome man dressed in a crisp white suit, his long hair framing a face with piercing blue eyes and a sharp nose. He stepped into the house, a rolled newspaper in hand, his gaze fixed on Sunehri. With an easy confidence, he settled onto the sofa across from her.

"Suni, sit," he said, his voice deep and steady, gesturing to the armchair in front of him. Mrs. Goswamy blinked, taken aback by the stranger's familiarity, but Sunehri, unruffled, met his eyes and sank into the chair without hesitation.

"I'm so sorry about your husband, my friend," he said softly, waving the newspaper in his hand. Before he could continue, Vivék darted to Sunehri's side. She subtly raised a hand, signaling the man to hold off on that topic in front of her son.

"Kaun hai yeh, beti?" Mrs. Goswamy asked in Hindi, her curiosity piqued.

"He's my classmate, Ma," Sunehri replied. "We graduated together from the University of Pennsylvania."

"Just a moment—I'll get some coffee," Mrs. Goswamy offered, turning toward the kitchen.

"No, thank you, Maaji," he said politely, rising from the sofa. "I just flew in from London for a business conference and have to leave soon." He looked at Sunehri. "Suni, I'd like to speak with you privately. Could I have your phone number?"

"Hold on," she said, retrieving her bulky mobile phone. She gave him her number and jotted his down in return.

"I'll call you this evening," he promised, then bent to ruffle Vivék's hair. "What a bright little guy." He strode toward the door, pausing to add, "Let me know, Suni—I'll meet you again at the Amar Jawan Jyoti shrine."

"Sure," she nodded.

"I'm here to help," he called as he hurried to the car, "anytime you need me."

A wave of relief washed over Sunehri, her classmate's genuine kindness easing the weight of her grief. She resolved to press on with her solitary journey, driven by her love for Vivék and the cherished memories of Raju. She vowed to shield her son from her sorrow until he was old enough to understand the world's harsh realities. Having faced the nightmare every soldier's wife dreads, she steeled herself to confront whatever lay ahead.

* * *

To unravel why Raju turned into an atheist and ultimately lost his sense of self, we must delve into his past—and determine whether he truly was a murderer. Born in London, Raju was the son of Ramnath and Diana, both archaeologists. Ramnath's father, Dharmaraju—Raju's grandfather—was a freedom fighter and landlord in the remote village of Madhurapudi on Andhra Pradesh's east coast. He fiercely opposed his younger son's marriage to Diana, a British woman, especially after the British government seized his 150 acres of farmland during World War II to build an airport, compensating him with a pittance. Enraged, Dharmaraju banished the couple from the village, disinherited Ramnath by donating his share of the estate to a welfare trust, and died shortly after. Ramnath's childless elder brother, Ishwar, stood to inherit the family's vulnerable wealth. To secure it, Ramnath entrusted his infant son to Ishwar, swearing him to secrecy about the boy's true parentage. Ramnath and Diana then returned to London, leaving their child behind.

Ishwar named the boy Dharma Raju in a ceremonial rite, raising him as his own. Raju grew up believing Ishwar was his father, unaware of the truth locked in his uncle's heart. He never saw his real parents again. At six, Raju learned of the wealth and land Ishwar had set aside for him. But in 1971, the Indian government's Land Reforms Act stripped landlords of holdings over 18 acres, plunging Ishwar's family into hardship and affecting the farmers who relied on him. To shield his assets, Ishwar transferred temporary rights to his accountants, only to be betrayed and lose everything.

In secret, Ishwar wrote to Ramnath and Diana, updating them on Raju's life, though he never expected replies—any response risked exposing the truth if Raju stumbled upon it.

Raju was sharp and perceptive, quick to grasp the world around him. Ishwar insisted he study English and Sanskrit—languages bridging the modern and ancient worlds—and the Vedas for spiritual depth. Raju embraced these lessons, growing fascinated by self-realization and the mysteries of existence.

One morning, as the sun cast golden rays over the lawn, Ishwar and Raju stepped out for a walk. "My son," Ishwar began, his voice tinged with melancholy.

"Yes, Father?" Raju replied, sensing his unease.

Ishwar pulled a leather pouch from his coat, revealing a copper foil etched with ancient Telugu script.

"What's that, father?" Raju asked, peering at it curiously.

"It's our family's history," Ishwar said, unrolling it. "Our lineage stretches back to 14th century. It begins with Perumaal from Addanki province; he was a vassal to King Prataparudra. Our ancestors moved to the east after the fall of Vijayanagara. They were generous souls—your grandfather, Dharmaraju, even donated land for the village school." He showed Raju a document bearing Dharmaraju's signature: Dharmaraju – The Landlord. "We must uphold his legacy, son. God favors those who serve others."

"Does God exist, father?" Raju snapped, his tone sharp with doubt.

"Of course He does," Ishwar replied calmly, a faint smile breaking through.

"Is He human?"

"No, He's beyond that."

"Then who is He?"

"He's eternal—perhaps Nature itself," Ishwar said gently. "He works wonders for us. This world is His creation."

"Prove it," Raju challenged, frustration bubbling up. He needed answers, not vague assurances.

"God's existence is debated—believed by some, denied by others. We can't prove Him physically unless He wills it," Ishwar explained.

"When will I see Him?"

"There are two paths," Ishwar said. "First, seek Him within through meditation, goodness, and standing against evil. Only then can you glimpse Him in nature. The second is liberation—Moksha."

"I trust you, Father, so I'll believe God exists," Raju said, though his voice carried a hint of resentment. "But why aren't we happy?"

"A diamond endures more pressure than a gem," Ishwar replied, pausing to gather his thoughts. Raju's relentless questions unsettled him. How could he distill God's grandeur into words a child could grasp? His own certainty wavered under the boy's scrutiny.

"Should we help others even when we're busy, if we're able?" Raju pressed.

"Yes," Ishwar said firmly. "Protecting those in need is the highest virtue. The Vedas say: *Swaashritaavana samoonahi dharmaha.*" He handed Raju a gold-edged Bhagavad Gita. "Remember this verse: *Yadihaasthi thadanyathra yannehaasti nathath kvachith*—what exists here exists everywhere; what doesn't, exists nowhere."

Raju felt a flicker of joy holding the sacred gift, but confusion lingered. His father's spiritual fervor and odd demeanor left him questioning, caught between awe and doubt.

* * *

That afternoon, Ishwar dialed his childhood friend, Mukhesh Ghosh, an army major who had chosen a life of service over marriage. The two had studied together at Calcutta University until their pre-university course. Ishwar invited Mukhesh to spend the summer at his home, but Mukhesh, tied up with the looming Indo-Pak conflict, promised to visit during Pongal instead. Ishwar had other intentions: he wanted to entrust Raju to Mukhesh for his education and to prepare him for the future. When Mukhesh eventually traveled to South India to see his old friend, he learned of Ishwar's plan and agreed wholeheartedly. Under Mukhesh's guidance, Raju blossomed into a skilled soldier, forging strong bonds with his comrades at the border, where tensions were, for a time, manageable.

Yet Raju often found himself wrestling with silent questions: Why is God toying with me like this? Who am I? What am I? No answers came, though he never anticipated how swiftly they would arrive. Life had begun as a tangle of threads, but Mukhesh, whom Raju came to see as a godfather, gave it direction. With

Mukhesh's support, Raju married Sunehri, Mukhesh's radiant niece, and found a happiness that erased the shadows of his past. Time sped by in a blur of joy, his wife anchoring his heart, their union yielding a son, Vivék.

Now, with five-year-old Vivék perched on his lap, Raju noticed the boy's distant gaze. It was hard to tell if Vivék grasped the gravity of their situation, though he seemed to sense something was wrong. Raju's mind drifted to his own childhood, to a day when Ishwar patiently answered his theological musings—much like this moment. Had the conflict not erupted, Raju would have been home in Delhi with Sunehri and Vivék by June 4, planning to return to base on June 21. But one truth burned clear: I was born to fight for my country. Mukhesh, despite his higher rank, admired Raju's dedication and sincerity, often praising his efforts.

The Indo-Pak conflict escalated, and the Indian government ordered the army to crush terrorist forces encroaching on Kashmir. Raju, now a Lieutenant Colonel in the Border Security Force, led a unit into the fray. The battle raged along the Line of Control, a tempest of chaos unfolding that night. Thunder roared, drowned out by the deafening blasts of air-to-ground missiles, while a storm of bullets cut through the air sharper than the rain. Lightning ignited the grassy fields, reducing them to ash as soldiers fell, sacrificing their lives for the nation. The Indian forces pressed northwest, determined to reclaim their land. Brigadier Mukhesh deployed every unit under his command to the front.

"Raju, stay close!" Mukhesh's voice boomed with authority.

"Yes, sir," Raju replied instantly, unwilling to abandon the man who had become his rock—the last person who truly cared for him.

"This chaos will pass soon," Mukhesh said, his tone taut with strain.

"Is that true, sir?" Raju asked, a mix of hope and frustration in his voice. "This sudden challenge has me on edge!"

"It's what every soldier faces," Mukhesh replied, his words firm yet warm. "Give it your all—but stay cautious. Don't cross the Line of Control."

"Understood, sir. Take care of yourself," Raju said respectfully, his obedience unwavering.

After their exchange, Raju moved out, marching a short distance with his troop. He relied on cutting-edge wireless tech to coordinate with his men, scanning the horizon for threats. He advanced through the burning fields, firing at enemy combatants until his ammunition ran dry. Then, without warning, a wave of militant shock troops and suicide bombers breached the border, storming the army camp in a ferocious assault. The camp was thinly defended—most soldiers had pushed into enemy territory to strike at bunkers, leaving the remainder unprepared for the onslaught. The militants unleashed a barrage of gunfire, sweeping through the

Indian ranks like a merciless tide, their sights set on Brigadier Mukhesh.

Raju, sensing danger, raced back to Brigadier Mukhesh's bivouac just as an armed figure darted toward it. Instinctively identifying the man as a terrorist, Raju gave chase across the rugged terrain. After a tense pursuit, he cornered the fleeing assailant, and a brutal fistfight erupted between them.

But the terrorist swiftly snatched the 9mm pistol from Raju's pocket—his last weapon—and shoved him aside. Raju stumbled, crashing to the muddy ground, then scrambled back, grabbing a stray revolver he spotted nearby. He pulled the trigger, but it clicked uselessly— no bullets. Twenty yards apart, both men squared off, weapons raised. Mukhesh, witnessing the standoff, sprinted toward them to shield Raju, ignoring his shouts to stay back. The terrorist fired. Raju tried to return fire, but his revolver failed again. In a split second, Mukhesh leaped between them, taking the bullet meant for Raju. It struck his head, and he crumpled lifeless to the earth.

"No!" Raju screamed, rushing to Mukhesh's side, cradling Mukhesh's body.

A bolt of lightning tore through the sky, striking the terrorist with blinding force. He erupted in flames, darted into the steep valley bellow. The rain ceased abruptly, washing away the chaos, leaving Raju alone on the sodden battlefield with Mukhesh's body.

Soldiers nearby, misinterpreting the scene, assumed Raju had shot the Brigadier—they hadn't seen the terrorist fire. They encircled him, weapons drawn.

"Shoot him!" the Colonel barked, his voice thick with venom.

"No, sir!" a soldier cried, stepping in front of Raju. It was Major Kushwanth Singh, his friend. But the troop opened fire without hesitation, riddling Kushwanth with bullets. The force flung him back into Raju, knocking them both to the ground.

Reeling from the impact, Raju staggered backward, his foot catching a rock at the plateau's edge. He tumbled headlong down the rain-slicked slope, sliding into the valley below and disappearing into the dense Himalayan cedar forest.

"Colonel, sir, he can't survive down there," a Jawan said, peering into the abyss. "If he's alive, he's barely hanging on."

"I won't let him escape," the Colonel spat, his words laced with envy over Raju's rapid rise. "He's a traitor. Search the valley. If he's dead, tell the media I killed him when the war's over."

The soldiers descended the treacherous ravine without ropes, a grueling hour-long trek. They scoured the area but found no sign of Raju—only a single boot, a revolver, and bloodstains trailing into the jungle.

"Colonel, sir!" a Jawan reported through his microphone. "He's likely dead. No trace of him. Leopards might've taken him."

"Fine," the Colonel replied curtly. "Come back up. Bring whatever he left behind."

* * *

In the darkness, faint sounds reverberated—beeping, the snip of scissors near his head, and a jumble of voices, some mentioning a person but too muddled to discern. Nothing felt real, neither pain nor relief, just a vague limbo.

"He's coming around," an unfamiliar voice remarked. "Only two days—he's tougher than I thought. I figured it'd take at least a few more."

"Eight fractures across his body," another voice chimed in, clinical and detached. "Two are critical, and they're still bleeding."

Raju's eyelids fluttered open. A blinding light glared down from above, forcing him to squint. He tried to sit up, but his body refused to obey; even turning his head was impossible. With effort, he shifted his gaze leftward, catching sight of several figures in black masks. As his vision cleared, they resolved into doctors, one distinguished by a stethoscope draped around his neck.

"Where am I?" Raju murmured, the words slipping out instinctively. "Who saved me?"

"We did," the stethoscope-wearing man replied calmly.

"We who?" Raju pressed, his voice weak but insistent.

"You shouldn't be talking," the man said, his tone firm yet measured. "You're in critical condition. Full recovery could take a long time."

Raju's mind churned, piecing together a fragmented understanding. He sensed a purpose in his survival—God, or fate, had spared him from death's grasp, not out of mercy, but to test his endurance, transforming a violent end into a grueling confinement. It had to be for his family, he reasoned, the only anchor left to him.

Time blurred into an indistinct haze. The mysterious figures kept him sedated, sustaining him with IV drips. Day and night lost meaning; he couldn't tell how long he'd been there. Whenever he mustered the strength to ask who they were or where he was, their responses were cryptic, evasive, leaving him adrift in uncertainty.

2

A thrifty plan of the God

A car sped through a crossroad in the predawn stillness, halting beside a concrete bench on the sidewalk. Two muscular men in tracksuits stepped out from the front, flung open the rear door, and hauled out a limp but well-dressed figure.

Unconscious, the man's arms draped over their shoulders as they dragged him to the bench, propping him upright before vanishing into the fading night. As dawn broke, the road buzzed with life, and Raju jolted awake, bewildered, to find an elderly man beside him flipping through a weekly magazine.

"What is this place?" Raju asked, his voice groggy. "How did I get here?"

"Hmm… maybe you had one too many last night," the old man chuckled, shutting the magazine. "This is Delhi. Never seen you around here before."

Raju's eyes flicked to the magazine's cover, freezing as he registered the date: June 2011. "Twelve years…" he muttered, stunned. "How did I lose twelve years in some unknown place? I need to find my wife…"

He sprang up, rummaging through his pockets, and pulled out six hundred-rupee notes and two thousand-rupee notes—cash planted by his mysterious escorts. As he wandered, he marveled at India's transformation over the past decade: a booming economy, soaring prices, and sprawling urban growth. Yet some pockets lingered unchanged, steeped in poverty reminiscent of the Appalachian backwoods.

After what felt like an eternity, Raju reached his old home. Peering at the familiar semidetached house, he slipped through the gate, pressed the doorbell, and waited, heart pounding. The knob turned, and his excitement surged—only to crash when the door swung open. A stranger stood there, not Sunehri or Vivék. The house had new occupants.

"Who are you?" Raju demanded. "Can you call my wife, Sunehri?"

"No idea who that is," the man replied curtly. "We've lived here three years. Mrs. Ganga Goswamy rented it to us."

Without a word, Raju bolted to Mrs. Goswamy's house, certain she'd recognize him. He hammered on her door, urgency driving his fists.

"Who's there?" a frail voice called from within, trembling with age. "Hold on—I'm not 18 anymore, I'm 80! I can't sprint!"

The door creaked open, and an old woman emerged, her eyes widening in disbelief.

"I'm… Raju…" he began, bracing for her to have forgotten him.

"Raju, you're alive!" she gasped. "We thought you were dead! How are you, my boy?"

"I'm fine, Mrs. Goswamy," he said, steadying himself. "Where's Sunehri? Why did you think I was dead?"

"The army listed you among the soldiers killed in the war," she explained, her face lighting up as she studied him. "Sunehri left this house ten years ago. Said she was moving to London with a classmate."

"London…?" Raju echoed, disappointment sinking in. "Do you have her contact?"

"She didn't leave an address or number," Mrs. Goswamy sighed. "I think she wanted to cut ties with this country, living with your memory."

"I need to see her," Raju said, voice tight with resolve.

"What now?" she asked.

"I'll go to London within five months," he declared.

"But how will you afford a ticket?"

"I'll find a job," he said, turning toward the gate. "See you again, Mrs. Goswamy!"

"Where are you off to, son?"

"Looking for a rental."

"No," she insisted. "Stay here if you'd like!"

"No, thanks—"

"Please, Raju beta!" she urged. "Stay until you leave for London!"

"Alright," he relented, smiling. "Thank you, Maa. Now I need a job."

"Beta," she said softly.

"Yes?" he nodded.

"I've got a little surprise," she said, hurrying to her prayer room and returning with a small box. "Sunehri left this for you before she went. I never opened it."

Raju peeled back the wrapping, his breath catching as he uncovered a Bhagavad Gita—the gold-edged copy his father, Ishwar, had gifted him, his sole inheritance, preserved for him all these years.

"This must be Paramaathma's plan," Mrs. Goswamy said with a knowing smile. "Your life's about to shift, aligning with your deepest desires. You'll see your family soon."

"Daadima!" a brash voice bellowed from the living room. "New face in the house? Who's this?"

"Come here, Vijju, meet our guest," she called back.

A stocky guy of 21 with a biker's swagger burst in. "Uncle Raju!" he exclaimed, grinning. "Vivék and I were best buds as kids. I've missed him for a decade!"

* * *

Countless tourists from across the globe gathered around the Taj Mahal, snapping photos of the marble masterpiece framed by its Eden-like Mughal garden. At the garden's heart, a long, narrow marble water tank—Hawd al-Kawthar, the Tank of Abundance—mirrored the Taj's ethereal beauty in its sapphire depths.

Among them stood Alexa, a striking Anglo-American archaeologist with copper-black hair and warm brown eyes. She'd been exploring Agra for a week with her five-person team, captivated by India's ancient wonders. Now, beside the tank, she photographed the monument, driven by a quest to uncover the hidden truths behind India's epic tales and a longing to meet the Himalayan saints.

Having traversed much of the eastern world to study ancient temples, she and her team were set to depart for Delhi that night, planning a two-day stay to research the old city independently—despite looming threats from shadowy forces.

The next morning, Raju awoke in Mrs. Goswamy's house, the unfamiliar surroundings stirring a sense of renewal.

He retrieved The Times of India from the floor and flipped through it, hunting for job listings. On the last page, a small ad caught his eye:

'MISSING CAR'

BMW D L 4900, silver 2009 750Li 7-Series sedan, black-tinted mirrors, valued at $80,300, missing since yesterday. $3,000 reward for information.
Contact: Yogi Raj Industries Pvt. Ltd., Red Fort Road, Delhi. Cell: 9868366883; 9397912229.

Raju's pulse quickened. This could be his ticket to London. He jotted down the details, muttering, "Why list it like a sales pitch?"

"Come, Raju beta, breakfast's ready!" Mrs. Goswamy called from the dining hall. "What have you been eating all these years? I made your favorite dosa today!"

After eating, he borrowed Vijju's motorbike and rode off to job-hunt. At that same moment, Alexa ventured alone to the Red Fort. Pausing at a crossroad to wait for her team, she was suddenly accosted by a gang of thugs wielding sharp weapons. Unarmed save for her camera, she bolted as a bike's horn blared nearby, sprinting toward the sound.

It was Raju, cruising down the Red Fort bypass. Alexa darted into his path, and he screeched to a halt, sizing up the situation. The thugs closed in, but Raju planted himself between them and her. "Stop, you bastards!" he growled, hoping they'd heed him. "This isn't our culture—harassing women, disrespecting a guest!"

They lunged instead. "I've been itching to thrash some unjust for years," Raju warned. "Today's my day!" He leaped off the bike, delivering a fierce kick to one thug's head, slamming another to the ground, and catching a swinging rod midair to smash its wielder's face into his knee. In seconds, the gang scattered, fleeing in defeat.

"Thank you, sir!" Alexa stammered, eyeing him warily.

"Don't worry, they're gone," Raju reassured her, noting her shaken expression. "Where are you staying?"

"I'm not local," she replied. "I'm here with my archaeology team. We're off to London tomorrow."

"Call your team—let them know we're here," he said briskly.

"May I have your name, sir? Are you police?" she asked, tilting her head.

"Not quite," he chuckled. "I'm Raju, ex-Lieutenant Colonel, Indian Army."

"Wow!" Alexa grinned, extending her hand. "I'm Alexa!" They shook hands, sharing a warm laugh.

"Pleasure to meet you," Raju said. "Here's my card— visit me if you're ever in London!"

"I'm headed there in a few months," he added confidently. "I'll look you up."

Her team rolled up in a cab. Alexa recounted the ordeal and introduced Raju. "See you soon, Mr. Raju!" she called, climbing in. "Bye!" they chorused as the cab pulled away. Raju waved, a gut feeling whispering this wasn't goodbye.

He stopped at the zebra crossing, the red signal started glowing. Then, a sleek silver sedan—matching the ad's description—flashed by. Raju gunned the bike, weaving through traffic to pursue it to the city's edge. A sallow-skinned man in a black jerkin drove the BMW. "Stop, or I'll end you!" Raju shouted, adrenaline surging. The driver smirked, veering onto a narrow road. Raju tailed him, lunging to grab his shoulder and landing a solid punch. "Drive where I tell you!" he barked.

The sedan screeched up to a colonial-style bungalow with a pagoda-like tower. Raju parked the bike in the front yard, stormed after the driver, and tackled him. As he pummeled the man, two guards in black suits emerged.

"We'll take him, sir," they said, dragging the driver off. "Please, go inside."

Raju stepped through the open door into a grand hall—marble floors, sky-blue walls adorned with scenic paintings, chandeliers glinting above intricate wooden carvings. Glass-railed stairs spiraled upward, and bronze

Bhakti Movement statues lined the space. "Hello? Anyone here?" he called, tense.

"Excuse me, sir," a shaky voice replied. A man in a pale coat and loose pants appeared. "Mr. Yogi will be down in ten minutes—he's meditating upstairs. Please sit."

"Thank you," Raju said, settling into a black armchair.

Fifteen minutes later, footsteps descended the staircase. A tall, striking man in a black suit appeared—over forty, jet-black hair to his shoulders, piercing blue eyes, with chiseled features. "Welcome to my villa, Mr…?"

"Raju, ex-Lieutenant Colonel, Border Security Force," he replied, standing. "You're Mr. Yogi?"

Yogi nodded. "Indeed. I admire your bravery."

"Pleasure to meet you," Raju said coolly. "You're a good meditator, I guess?"

"Thank you," Yogi smiled, gesturing to the chair. "Meditation fuels my success." Raju sat.

"What kind?" he asked. "You seem like a true yogi."

"Don't flatter me," Yogi laughed. "I'm just an art collector. I practice Kriya Yoga—it's my path to nirvana."

"Impressive," Raju said. "I've heard of it in the army."

"I've a surprise for you," Yogi teased. "Guess what?"

"My reward, of course," Raju grinned.

"I'll arrange it," Yogi said, eyes gleaming. "But my mission's just begun—I'm chasing a triumphant era!"

"Mission?" Raju pressed, intrigued yet wary. "What's that mean?"

"Some things defy words," Yogi began, then paused. "I'll explain in London."

"London?" Raju frowned. "Why there?"

"Your reward's waiting there," Yogi said, grinning. "Will you join me?"

Raju met Yogi's intense gaze, sensing secrets beneath it. Mrs. Goswamy's words about the Bhagavad Gita echoed—this was no coincidence. "Yes," he said, awestruck.

"You're sure?" Yogi asked, voice steady. "I don't break deals."

"I'm in," Raju confirmed, seeing his chance to find Sunehri and Vivék.

"Great! We've got an evening flight," Yogi said, rising. "Meet me this afternoon—I assume you've got luggage?"

"I do," Raju nodded. "I borrowed a friend's bike."

"Take your time," Yogi replied.

Raju sped back to Mrs. Goswamy's, returning the bike to Vijju. "What's wrong, Raju?" she asked, noting his haste.

"I'm off to London," he said, recounting the day.

"When will you return, Uncle Raju?" Vijju asked.

"Not until I'm with Sunehri and Vivék," he vowed.

He took a taxi to Yogi's villa, where men loaded bags into a car. Yogi waited inside. "Hurry, Raju, we've got a 5 p.m. deadline with this traffic!" he urged. They caught a 6:50 p.m. flight, landing in London the next morning.

3

Job becomes difficult

A cool breeze swept through London, carrying the fresh scent of rain that had washed over the city before dawn. As they stepped down from the airliner and walked towards the airport's main entrance, Yogi turned to Raju and greeted him warmly.

"Welcome to London, Mr. Raju," he said, before casting a glance to his left. Someone was waiting for them in the lounge.

"Come on, Raju. My men are waiting for us," Yogi continued as they left the cloakroom. He introduced Raju to the group.

"Hey Jason, meet Mr. Raju, our new teammate," Yogi said.

"We're all glad to meet you, Mr. Raju!" Jason responded as they exchanged handshakes.

Soon after, they made their way to Yogi's villa in Mary Yard, London.

As Raju entered the villa's vicinity, he heard the distant neighing of horses. His curiosity led him to a lush green polo field, where riders on horseback wielded long-handled mallets, driving a ball towards the goalposts. Yogi, without hesitation, joined the game, playing energetically through a chukka. Raju watched, astonished.

"Come on, Mr. Raju!" Yogi called out, beckoning him. "Have a ride!"

"Sure," Raju replied, mounting a sleek black horse.

"This is my polo team," Yogi explained. "We're training for the upcoming world championship!"

"That's impressive," Raju said, admiring Yogi's talent.

"Thank you, Mr. Raju," Yogi responded with a charming smile. His elegance and confidence left Raju deeply impressed. As they rode along the field, Yogi turned to him with a serious expression.

"Mr. Raju, if you don't mind, I'd like to ask you something."

Raju nodded, resting his left palm on his thigh with a sense of unease.

"Why did you agree to come here without hesitation when I asked you yesterday?" Yogi inquired firmly.

"My wife and son are here. I have to find them," Raju confessed, revealing his past to Yogi.

Yogi nodded thoughtfully. "Alright, Raju, I'll help you, but give me three months. London is like an ocean—it's hard to find a small fish in it. In the meantime, would you like a job here?"

"What kind of job, Mr. Yogi?" Raju asked.

"I arranged a position for you as a security guard at the British Museum," Yogi replied.

Raju hesitated. "But how can I—?"

"No need to worry," Yogi interrupted. "I'll provide you with a car, and you'll stay with me in this villa. Take your time and decide. Let me know tomorrow."

After a moment of contemplation, Raju made his decision. "I'll do it! I want to take this opportunity."

Yogi's face lit up. "Great! You'll start tomorrow and officially begin work on Monday. But I suggest you familiarize yourself with the Egyptian sculptures in Room 4 and the Indian sculptures in Room 33A."

"You've given me a new start, and I won't waste it," Raju said gratefully. Yet, a lingering thought gnawed at him—why was Yogi investing so much in him? He resolved to trust Yogi but remained determined to find his family.

A few days later, Raju joined the National History Museum. The security-in-chief, James Thomson, and his team welcomed him warmly.

"Hello, Mr. Raju!" James greeted him in a cheerful tone. He was a middle-aged man with sallow skin, brown hair, a sharp nose, and honey-colored eyes.

"Thank you! I'm honored to be here, Mr. James," Raju responded enthusiastically. "Would you tell me more about this museum?"

"Of course! Follow me to my office," James said.

The two walked briskly down the corridor and entered a room painted in blue and milky white, adorned with elegant tapestries. James gestured for Raju to sit.

"I'll give you some details about the museum," James began, his fingers clasped on the desk. "But some matters are classified."

"What do you mean?" Raju asked curiously.

"Certain aspects of this museum are secret. We must proceed with discretion," James said in a hushed tone.

Raju nodded but felt a surge of questions bubbling in his mind. What could be so secretive? Why was James being so cautious?

"Sir, I have a question about Room 4," Raju said suddenly.

"Ah, the Egyptian sculptures?" James responded.

"Yes."

James took a deep breath. "That's exactly what I was going to tell you. This involves a matter beyond ordinary comprehension. Do you know of Nebkheperure, also known as Tutankhamun?"

"Yes, he died at 19," Raju said confidently.

James leaned forward. "His death wasn't natural. He was assassinated by his own kin over a hidden treasure."

Raju listened intently as James continued. "What I'm about to tell you concerns a mysterious artifact—a capstone."

"What kind of artifact?" Raju asked.

"A capstone is a small yet powerful crystal placed atop pyramids to channel cosmic energy. This one, however, has been lost for over five millennia. It possesses immense power—to control, create, restore, innovate, generate, and even destroy."

Raju's pulse quickened. "Are you saying this capstone is in Room 4?"

"Precisely. And that's why I must warn you," James said gravely. "This is no ordinary object."

A moment of silence passed before Raju spoke again. "Mr. James, why are you telling me this? And how do you know all this?"

James hesitated, then sighed. "Because I believe you are the right person to understand this truth. My knowledge comes from my grandfather—an archaeologist who worked in Egypt between 1921 and 1939. He was part of the team that discovered Tutankhamun's tomb, alongside Lord Carnarvon and Howard Carter. My grandfather recorded secrets about the capstone in his journal."

James' voice grew solemn. "My father dismissed it as nonsense, but I knew better. And now, you must know too."

"I pressed him relentlessly until he finally relented and revealed those secrets. Since then, Egypt has rooted itself firmly in my thoughts," James said.

"Mr. James, will you share that secret with me?" Raju asked, a spark of excitement urging him to unravel the mystery.

"Of course," James replied with a nod. "What I'm about to tell you ties the Indo-Egyptian civilizations together."

He began: "Legend places this tale just before the dawn of Kaliyuga, the Dark Age, on February 17, 3102 BCE—1,778 years before King Tut's assassination. Among India's non-royal figures, one stands out: Kesika, who lived from 3139 to 3102 BCE. So renowned is he that he ranks among the world's most famous ancients. His name, though not his full identity, echoes through time, veiled in dark magic inscriptions rather than sacred texts. Kesika—meaning 'he who rises with Kundalini-shakti,' the dormant serpent power coiled at the base chakra beneath the coccyx—was long dismissed as myth by scholars. That changed in the late 19th century when evidence confirmed his existence. Hailing from CambhoojaRajya, part of the ancient Indian continent now known as Cambodia, he chased alchemy, mentored dark wizards worldwide, and a polymath: physician, scribe, astrologer, and high priest of the sun god Surya Dev.

"Kesika seized the throne of Uttunga, CambhoojaRajya's capital, by murdering its emperor and ruled for a decade. Yet today, his fame pales beside Vishnusamhita—a breathtaking princess from a lost continent south of India, often linked to the eastern Lemuria. A formidable sorceress, she spurned Kesika's marriage proposal, choosing instead Vivékadeva, a prince of Bharatavarsha whose name means 'lord of virtue.' A master of transcendental meditation and Kayakalpa—a yogic art of immortality—Vivékadeva wielded an emerald sword imbued with a possessive curse: its bearer was compelled to kill those nearby. But Vivékadeva's disciplined mind tamed its power, shielding him from delusion.

"Kesika invaded Lemuria to claim Vishnusamhita and its throne, but Vivékadeva battled him fiercely to protect her. In defeat, he cursed Kesika, reducing his body to ashes. Undeterred, the wizard's mastery allowed him to resurrect his astral form in an effulgent ring of light. He retaliated by hexing Vivékadeva, stealing the sword, and imprisoning him alive within a massive crystal idol.

"Witnessing this horror, Vishnusamhita chose Kapaalamoksha—self-liberation beyond nirvana. Awakening her Kundalini, she channeled its electric surge through her six chakras—Muulaadhaara to Aagna—merging the three naadis: Ed'a, Pingala, and

Shushumna. As the energy pierced her Brahmarandhra, the Sahasraarachakra's golden lotus bloomed, blasting a hole in her skull with a rocket-like thud. Her body stilled, blood and light pouring from the breach as her prana departed. Enraged at losing her, Kesika unleashed his cosmic might, raising the sea to swallow Lemuria into the Indian Ocean.

"But his ethereal form couldn't endure. He tasked his alchemist disciples with crafting *Spatika'dhaatu*, a tiny, triangular crystal to harness cosmic radiation. Before his Egyptian apprentice, Ka, Kesika performed a final act of magic, entrusting him with Vivékadeva's sword— guarded by Uruk's demons—and revealed a divine secret: 'Whoever masters this sword can use this crystal as a pyramid's capstone at a 52-degree angle, gaining supreme power and preserving my essence by reincarnating me within them.' Then, Kesika fused himself into the crystal.

"Ka, obsessed, slew 274 rivals to wield the sword and claim the capstone's power, but failed. Centuries later, in 2667 BCE, the Step Pyramid of Saqqara rose in Egypt, though it wasn't the first to bear a capstone. Pharaoh Sneferu's pyramid at Dahshur collapsed mid-construction, its angle reduced to 43 degrees, unfit for the crystal. We call it the Blunted Pyramid as it stood incomplete. Khufu's Great Pyramid of Cheops, topped with gold instead, left the crystal's fate unclear—perhaps he didn't build it, or rejected its alien aura.

"Some Egyptians revered the stone as a divine idol with world-dominating power, yet cursed: placed in the Great Pyramid's king's chamber, it could grant immense strength but drive its wielder mad or destroy those who sought to shatter it. Tutankhamun, wary of its chaos, planned its destruction but was assassinated in 1324 BCE, marking Egypt's downfall.

"Four millennia later, that capstone resurfaced last week in a cenotaph after a three-year search by nearly a hundred archaeologists. It's headed to our museum. Now, power-hungry fools chase it, though I doubt its legend holds water—it's unproven even today."

James laid out the tale with clarity, leaving Raju both captivated and skeptical of the ancient stone's mystique.

"Does anything out there actually talk about Lemuria existing?" Raju asked, leaning forward slightly.

"Yeah, we've got some clues," James said, scratching his chin. "Apart from Vivékadeva's story, the mentions of Kavaatapuram—Lemuria's capital— can be found in the Ramayana and Silappadhikaram. The thing is, Vivékadeva lived around Krishna's time, so we're talking way back."

"So, you don't think he's still alive?" Raju said, tilting his head. "Like, maybe stuck under the ocean somewhere?"

James gave him a skeptical look. "Alive? Come on, Raju, that was thousands of years ago. How's anyone breathing down there? Kesika didn't just finish him off—he was smart about it. Trapping him in that crystal was his way of wiping him out slow and permanent."

"But what if someone got their hands on that power?" Raju asked, his voice edged with curiosity.

"Nah, not happening," James shot back, his brow furrowing. "That sword? Gone. Disappeared fifty years ago before it even made it here."

"No way," Raju said, eyes widening. "That's worse—it could be anywhere."

"Maybe," James said with a shrug. "But my guess? Thieves melted it down for the gold."

Raju let out a small breath. "Okay, that'd be a relief if they did."

"Exactly," James said, nodding.

"Can I check out Kesika's capstone?" Raju asked, perking up.

"You can, but not right now," James replied. "They're fixing up the north wing downstairs—no one's seeing it for at least a week."

"Have you gotten a look at it?"

"Nope," James said casually. "Word is, the British government's bringing it in next Monday."

"Didn't they start showing it off yesterday?" Raju asked, confused.

"That was just a fake," James explained, his voice tightening a bit. "We shut it down—security risks with the real deal. Let's call it a day here. Catch you tomorrow?"

"Sounds good," Raju said, heading for the door. He stopped short and turned back. "Hey, James—where's the capstone at right now?"

"Downing Street," James said, matter-of-fact.

"Wait, what?"

"No. 10 Downing Street—you know, where the Prime Minister lives," James clarified.

Raju blinked. "Hold up. We've got seventy armed guards here round the clock. Isn't that enough? Why stick it there?"

"It's about last year's break-in," James said, leaning in slightly. "That place is a fortress compared to here. We still haven't caught whoever did it, and we're not chancing it again."

"Makes sense," Raju said. "Thanks for breaking it down, James. Catch you later."

Walking away, Raju replayed the chat with James Thomson in his head. The ancient relics had turned into some kind of modern legal mess, but something else bugged him: Why'd Yogi put me here, at this museum?

Needing answers, he made a beeline for the London Library at 14 St James's Square, Mayfair. Inside the circular reading room, he dug into piles of books on Egyptian and Indian history. Hours passed, but nothing gave him the straight detail about the capstone—he was still in the dark.

* * *

Raju made his usual trip to Yogi's mansion. He stepped into the hall and hurried down the corridor where Jason, the sallow-skinned man, waited, looking jittery. "Come on, Mr. Raju! The boss is expecting you in the meeting room!" Jason said, his voice tight with worry.

Raju followed him into the room. Yogi sat there in a drab brown armchair, his face grim and tense. The odd vibe from both men threw Raju off. "Take a seat, Raju," Yogi said, his tone strange. "How's the new job treating you?"

"Pretty informative," Raju replied. "I'm doing alright."

"Find anything weird at the British Museum?" Yogi asked, lowering his voice.

"Not really," Raju said, dodging the truth.

Yogi leaned in. "But if I'm guessing right, James Thomson's already filled you in on that mysterious thing, hasn't he?"

"What?" Raju played dumb. "You mean the capstone?"

"Exactly," Yogi said, eyes narrowing. "So, where's it at now?"

"I heard it's at the Prime Minister's residence," Raju answered.

"No, Raju, James fed you a line," Yogi countered. "It's still in the museum's northern block."

"How do you know that?" Raju shot back, irritation creeping in. "What are you after?"

Raju's nerves flared as he locked eyes with Yogi's intense blue stare.

"Relax, Raju," Yogi said, softening a bit. "I'm just looking out for you—your job, your safety. That's all." His words hinted at some vague future trouble he wanted Raju to sidestep.

"What are you even talking about?" Raju snapped, exasperated. "I still don't get you—why all this?"

Yogi chuckled lightly. "Oh, Raju, you're too serious. I'm an art collector—shipping antiques to museums is my gig. You may leave now. Catch you later."

"See you tomorrow," Raju muttered, heading for the door, disappointment heavy in his chest.

Just then, a stocky guy stepped in as Raju left. "Hey, Ravi," Yogi greeted, handing him a small notebook.

"Look at that—Ravi shows up, Raju takes off," the sallow-skinned Jason quipped in a low rasp. Yogi stifled a laugh, keeping it from reaching Raju.

The next day, Raju clocked in and found James in his office, looking worn out and on edge. "Come in, Raju, sit down," James said, his voice dragging.

"What's up, James? You look beat," Raju noted.

"You've got a big task ahead," James replied, steadying himself.

"What's that?" Raju asked, tapping the desk lightly, brow creasing.

"You're guarding the capstone tonight," James said.

Raju's stress spiked. Night duty for that little stone? It threw him for a loop. "Wait, what? It's here now? Why'd you lie to me?" he pressed, suspicion flaring.

"Sorry, Raju," James said, wincing. "I didn't know when the museum decided to bring it in and kick off the exhibit. But this—it's a real test for you."

"By myself?" Raju asked, incredulous.

"No, you'll have three guards outside the room," James assured him.

Raju's gut churned. Why him for this pointless rock? Still, knowing how many coveted it, he nodded.

"Alright, James. I won't argue—I'll do my best." He left for lunch, unease simmering.

The evening faded into a quiet night. By 11 p.m., Raju was stationed in the wide, oblong hall where the capstone sat. Frost and mist blanketed the deserted streets outside, the temperature dipping below zero. The museum was a tomb of silence. Raju met the three guards assigned with him.

"Hey," he said, sizing them up as they introduced themselves.

"I'm Steve."

"I'm Jake."

"I'm Ravi."

They shook hands, but Raju froze at Ravi—the stout guy from Yogi's villa. He flicked on his flashlight, catching Ravi's face. "Hold up, Ravi. Didn't I see you at Yogi's place when I was leaving?"

"Yeah, that's right, sir," Ravi said with a sly grin.

It clicked for Raju—James's move made sense now. Hours later, Steve and Jake slipped out and returned armed, their faces hard. Without warning, they lunged at him. Raju drew his revolver, firing twice—hitting their legs. Jake staggered, then charged with a rifle. Raju's army instincts kicked in; a single shot dropped him. As he dodged the barrel, a sharp sting hit his neck—a tranquilizer dart from Ravi behind him.

"You bastard, Ravi!" Raju roared, fury boiling over as he blacked out and hit the floor.

They dragged him to a corner, binding him with thin metal wires and taping his mouth shut. The guards turned to the capstone's case, but Ravi hesitated. "No point in breaking it—laser security's too tight," he muttered. Instead, they looted Tutankhamun's ornaments and bolted.

Raju came to in the museum's hospital wing, groggy. "How you holding up?" the doctor asked softly.

"When can I get out?"

"Figured you'd ask," the doctor said with a faint smile. "Three weeks' rest. That was a nasty venom dart—lucky you pulled through."

Raju's eyes drifted to a framed quote in the corner:

I only give treatment…
He cures!

"Who?" Raju asked.

"God," the doctor said without missing a beat.

"No, I mean—who paid my bill?"

"Your relatives," came the slow reply.

Raju frowned. Relatives in London? No one visited him during those weeks. The robbery exploded across global media, TV crews clamoring for his story, but museum brass shut it down—his life stayed unchanged.

Officials grilled him: "What went down that night before you getting knocked down?" He couldn't pinpoint it, just laid out his suspicions—naming Yogi, though unsure why he'd want him dead. Aimless now, Raju's hope of finding Sunehri and Vivék in London flickered out.

4

Don't interrupt us

Three weeks later, Raju got discharged from the hospital and returned to the museum to inquire about job opportunities as the British Museum had announced they were rehiring former staff.

Raju casually strolled into James' office. The room had undergone a transformation—new decor and a different vibe greeted him.

"Hello! Anyone here? Mr. James!" Raju called out softly.

Silence answered him, but faint murmurs drifted from the doorway. Assuming someone was approaching, he tried again. "Hey… Mr. James!" His words faltered as a stranger stepped into the room.

"I thought Mr. James was coming! Who are you?" Raju asked, a mix of curiosity and unease in his tone.

The man fixed him with a puzzled stare. "I could ask you the same thing. Who are you?"

"I'm Raju. I've been a security guard here for the past three months."

"Oh, you're that guy!" the man replied, recognition dawning. "I heard you were out of commission for a few weeks. I'm Daniel Hamilton." His voice was low and rough, paired with a sly, unpleasant grin. Daniel was a stocky figure—round-faced, with small, squinting eyes and a stubby nose. Recently promoted from France, he carried himself with an air of arrogance and seemed oblivious to past events.

"Where's Mr. James Thomson?" Raju asked, irritation creeping into his voice.

"He quit," Daniel said smugly, clearly pleased with himself.

"But I was going to—" Raju began, only to be cut off.

"No chance of you working here. You're fired!" Daniel snapped, his tone sharp and dismissive.

Raju shook his head. "I actually came to resign. Looks like we're on the same page. I've decided to leave the country. Thanks for the respect, sir—I'm out of here."

As he left the museum, Raju couldn't shake the questions swirling in his mind. Why had James resigned so suddenly after the incident? Where was he now? The uncertainty gnawed at him.

His phone buzzed, interrupting his thoughts. He answered it.

"Hello, Mr. Raju!" came a deep, familiar voice. "How are you?"

"Why did you try to kill me?" Raju demanded, his frustration boiling over. "What's your game?"

"Kill you? No, no! And you're the one dragging my name into this," Yogi replied, dodging the accusation. "I've got bad news about your wife."

"What?" Raju's voice rose in anger. "How am I supposed to find her and my son in this huge city?"

"I heard they've gone back to India," Yogi said nonchalantly. "Sorry about that."

"Don't mess with me!" Raju roared. "Where in India are they?"

"No idea. Bye!" The line went dead.

"Wait!" Raju shouted, but it was too late. The slim thread of hope he'd clung to—that Yogi might help him locate his family—snapped. Months earlier, James had warned him, "I need to stop this from happening again."

Now, Raju was convinced Yogi was the mastermind behind his troubles.Determined to leave London without his wife and son, Raju stood on Montague Street, hailing a taxi to the airport.

He arrived around 10:30 PM and booked a second-class ticket to India. Though he considered visiting relatives before departing, the vastness of the city overwhelmed him, deepening his sense of despair.

"Attention, passengers: the flight to India is delayed by two hours due to adverse weather. Please remain patient," an announcement crackled over the speakers.

Raju sighed and headed to the cloakroom to reorganize his luggage. As he turned to leave, a woman at the counter called out, "Excuse me, sir, you need to pay for your ticket!"

"Right," he muttered, reaching for his wallet. To his dismay, it was gone—stolen sometime before he'd booked the ticket. Stranded in the bustling airport, he scanned the crowd for any sign of the thief, but no one stood out.

"May I have your attention?" a raspy voice said behind him. "Is something wrong, sir?"

Raju turned to see a lean young man, about twenty, with striking blue eyes, jet-black hair, and a sharp nose—slightly shorter than Raju himself.

Relieved by the Brit's concern, Raju nodded. "Yes, I'm Raju. Who are you?"

"I'm Henry Yates, nephew of Mr. Vijay, the Director of Antiquities," the boy replied with confidence. "I saw you at the museum a month ago. How do you know my name, though?"

"Nice to meet you, Henry," Raju said warmly. "I don't recall every visitor's face, to be honest."

"Fair enough. What's the issue? You look troubled," Henry pressed.

"I lost my wallet just now, and I need to get back to my country," Raju explained, his voice heavy with exhaustion.

"Come with me," Henry offered. "No need to argue—it's my duty. My uncle can arrange a first-class ticket for you."

"But it's pouring outside!" Raju protested.

"No worries, Mr. Raju. We'll take the car," Henry assured him.

The rain eased after a few minutes, and they headed to the parking lot after canceling Raju's ticket.

"Let's go!" Henry urged.

"Wait," Raju said. "Didn't you mention your sister arriving from LA soon? Shouldn't we pick her up?"

Henry nodded, but before he could respond, Raju's phone rang again. The screen flashed Yogi's name. Muttering to himself, Raju stepped aside as Henry scanned the crowd for his sister.

No one appeared. Suddenly, Henry felt a twitch in his back pocket. Whipping around, he spotted a girl— nineteen, copper-haired, slim, dressed in a hooded jacket and worn jeans—darting toward the exit. She matched Henry's height. Checking his pocket, he realized his wallet was gone too. She must have taken Raju's as well.

"What's wrong, Henry? Forget something?" Raju asked.

"Same as you!" Henry replied, pointing. "She stole our wallets! I'm going after her!"

"But you said we had a car?"

"The keys are with my sister, who's not here yet," Henry admitted. "I came on my skateboard."

Grabbing his board from his rucksack, Henry sped off after her. The girl hopped on a bicycle, weaving through traffic with alarming speed. She darted into an alley, turning left into a dead-end nook. Trapped, she screeched to a halt, her bike skidding slightly. Henry braked too, grazing the building's edge but regaining his footing as he approached her.

She stared at him, dazed and distant.

"Give me the wallet!" Henry demanded, his voice tight with anger.

She smirked faintly.

Furious, Henry lunged forward—just as she charged, landing a kick to his chest. He stumbled back, hitting the ground. As she aimed another blow, he dodged, rolling aside.

"I don't want to hurt you! Just hand it over," he pleaded.

"Oh, how sweet! Worried about me?" she taunted.

"Give it back!" he barked.

"Me? Oh no—AAH!" Her words cut off as Henry struck back, kicking her square in the face. She crashed into her bike, collapsing into the mud.

"TOM, Rogues! GARRY! NATE! ED!" she screamed, summoning her crew.

Moments later, a tall, copper-haired man rushed in, knocking Henry down with a brutal shove. Henry hit the ground hard.

"Emma, you okay?" the man asked, helping her up.

"Yeah, Tom," she replied, breathless. "He got me, but I'm fine—just some dirt. I tripped, then stomped back up."

Tom launched into action, leaping into the air with a flip, grabbing Henry's shoulder, and hurling him against the wall. Henry groaned, crumpling in pain. As he struggled to rise, Tom knelt beside him, gripping his throat with a vile grin and muttering crude threats.

"What the hell are you saying?" Henry spat, seething.

A silver sedan rolled slowly past the street's entrance.

"Don't mess with us—just mind your own business! Emma, give his wallet back!" Tom growled, issuing a command.

"Give me Raju's wallet too!" Henry shouted.

"What wallet? No chance. Stay out of our way, or you'll regret it," Tom warned.

"Again? What'll you do?" A sharp, commanding voice cut through the tension from the alley's entrance.

"Who's that?" Tom bellowed, spinning around.

Henry froze. It was his sister, Alexa—dressed in a sleek black outfit, her copper-black hair whipping in the breeze, shades perched on her striking face. She looked like a secret agent.

"I'm his sister," she declared.

"Looks like she's here to save him," one of the men muttered.

"Spot on, Nate," Emma said, eyeing Alexa warily.

"Emma, right? Cambridge University?" Alexa asked coolly, helping Henry to his feet. "Henry, step back."

She advanced toward them with the grace of a warrior.

"She's trouble," Emma whispered.

The group lunged at Alexa. She countered flawlessly—spinning into the air, kicking Tom in the neck, shoving Emma backward, and driving a fist into Ed's gut. The fight lasted three minutes.

Then, from her back pocket, she drew a revolver. Raising it skyward, she fired twice. The shots boomed through the alley, rattling everyone but Emma.

"Don't move!" Alexa ordered.

Emma's face glistened with sweat, her breathing ragged, her eyes locked on Alexa in tense silence.

"She's scared," Henry murmured.

"Why'd you try to kill my brother?" Alexa demanded.

"No! I didn't mean to kill him—we're after the Indian man!" Emma stammered, her voice shaky but honest.

"Why him?" Alexa pressed.

"I don't know! Yogi told me to nab his wallet," Emma blurted. "Your brother got in the way."

"Here's a tip," Alexa said icily. "You shouldn't be working for Yogi."

"What's that supposed to mean? He got me into Cambridge—said he'd back me up!" Emma shot back, bewildered.

"Where is he?" Alexa snapped.

"Not now. Meet me here in ten days—same time, same place. I'll talk then," Emma said, flustered.

Alexa and Henry left the alley, heading for the car.

"Give Raju his wallet," Alexa instructed.

"Damn it," Henry muttered, checking it. "It's empty."

"We should tell Uncle Vijay," Alexa suggested. "You in?"

"Yeah," Henry agreed. "How did you find me, Sis?"

"Raju tipped me off."

"What? You know him?" Henry asked, stunned.

"He saved my life in Delhi. Ex-Indian army. I saw him at the museum a month ago too—Uncle Vijay vouched for him. He even covered Raju's hospital bills. Plus, he was on the news—survived a robbery."

"How did he find you?" Henry pressed.

"At the airport. I bumped into him by the lounge. He recognized me instantly and said you'd chased after some girl. Embarrassing, huh?"

"You messing with me?" Henry grumbled.

"Nope," she replied. "Let's go home."

"Wait! I told Raju I'd take him to Uncle Vijay!" Henry remembered.

"Fine," Alexa sighed, nodding toward the car. Raju stood beside it, flashing them a grin.

"He's waiting," Henry noted.

"We both came for you," Alexa said, sliding into the car.

"Everything good, kids?" Raju asked.

"Yep," Alexa chirped. "Hop in, Mr. Raju—we're taking you to our place."

"Great!"

"Take a seat," Henry said, gesturing to the back.

"No, I'll drive," Raju insisted. "Just guide me."

He started the engine as they settled in. "Which way?"

"Right onto Vauxhall Bridge Road, left at John Islip Street, then straight to Westminster Bridge Road," Henry directed, pointing ahead.

Five minutes later, they pulled up to a stunning villa.

"Here we are!" Alexa sang out.

Raju parked and eyed the place. "This is your uncle's?"

"Yeah, come on in," Henry said.

They stepped into a drawing room adorned with stone carvings, elegant portraits, and four dark maple armchairs by a fireplace.

"Just wait," Alexa said. "I'll call Uncle Vijay." She darted off to the living room.

At that moment, Raju's gaze drifted to a portrait resting on the mantelpiece. A brown cat slinked along the hearth, brushing against the warm stones. Henry flopped into an armchair, exhaling deeply.

"Hello, Mr. Raju!" a rich, resonant voice called from behind him. "How are you holding up?"

Raju turned to see Vijay—a tall, imposing Brit in his sixties, exuding strength and poise. His piercing eyes gleamed like a cheetah's, set above a sculpted nose and framed by neatly trimmed brown hair. He carried an air of distinction and warmth that instantly put Raju at ease.

"Hello, Mr. Vijay! It's a pleasure to meet you," Raju replied, extending a hand.

"Likewise," Vijay said with a broad, genuine smile, clasping Raju's hand firmly. "Please, take a seat."

Raju settled into one of the sleek black armchairs, while Vijay sat across from him, his presence commanding yet approachable.

"Well done, Henry—great work!" Vijay said, his tone approving.

"What? I deserve the credit here!" Alexa interjected playfully, her voice light but insistent.

Vijay chuckled. "I'm not talking about that, actually. Henry staged quite the comeback, didn't he?"

"Yes, Mr. Vijay," Raju cut in, seizing the moment. "But I've lost everything—my licenses, my museum ID. If it's not too much trouble, could you help me retrieve them?" He pinned his hopes on Vijay, the last person he felt he could turn to.

Vijay nodded thoughtfully. "The wallet's not the real issue, though, is it? You seem weighed down by something deeper."

Raju sighed. "Yes, it's my family. I lost them ten years ago."

"Are they here now?" Vijay asked, leaning forward slightly.

"No. Yogi told me they've gone back to India."

"I'd wager he's lying," Vijay said, his voice firm. "Give me their details—I'll help you find them."

"Thank you!" Raju said, gratitude washing over him. Then, curiosity sparked. "Mr. Vijay, you're not Indian—how did you end up with a name like 'Vijay'?"

Vijay grinned, settling back in his chair. "Good question. I was born in Noida. My full name is Vincent Ian Johnson Adam Yates. My father was a district collector in India back in 1945. He fell in love with the country and its culture, so he nicknamed me Vijay. Now, I'm the Director of Antiquities." He shrugged lightly. "That's the story."

"Thanks for covering my hospital bill, Mr. Vijay," Raju added, his tone softening.

"Hey, it's my duty to help those in need," Vijay replied, locking eyes with Raju. "But I owe you thanks for saving Alexa."

"Of course," Raju said earnestly. "It's my duty to protect people too."

Vijay laughed, a warm, rumbling sound. "My apologies, Raju—I forgot who I was talking to for a moment."

"No worries, Mr. Vijay," Raju assured him with a small smile.

Raju carried a quiet strength, rooted in a deep sense of duty. His ambitions weren't driven by personal gain or self-interest—he'd never compromise his principles for them. Instead, he worked tirelessly, balancing his goals with the needs of those around him, a lifelong dance of purpose and sacrifice.

5

Alexa's effort

Raju's eyes lingered on Vijay's commanding face, a portrait of eminence seen clearly in his steady gaze. He trusted this man implicitly. "Alexa and Henry are remarkable young people," Raju said, his voice warm with admiration. "Where are their parents?"

Vijay leaned back, his gaze drifting briefly to the fire. "Their family once lived in New York. Now my brother, John, resides in LA."

Raju's brow furrowed, suspicion threading through his next question. "Mr. Vijay, how long have you known about Yogi? And what of Alexa's mother?"

"Hold on, Raju," Vijay said, raising a hand before turning to his niece. "Alexa, do you recall the World Trade Center disaster?"

Her expression tightened. "Yes, but why bring that up now?"

"Were you there when the towers fell?" Raju asked, his curiosity piqued.

Alexa nodded, her voice steady but shadowed with memory. "I'll never forget it. I saved a few children that day, but I lost my mom. She'd been running a website—www.monumentsarecorrupted.com—exposing   an archaeological mafia. It gained traction, huge success, really."

"What brought you there that day?" Raju pressed, leaning forward.

"She'd been promoted," Alexa began, her tone measured. "A top-tier computer hacker at the WTC, tasked with thwarting viruses and screening foreign emails. On September 11, 2001, she brought me to her office to see her work. It was 8:30 AM when she started sifting through a flood of emails. The General Manager was already on edge, barking at the engineers to focus. Then an anonymous email hit her inbox. Carelessly, she opened it, ignoring the system's warning about a virus. I peeked over her shoulder—inside was a chilling message: '09-11-01; WTC will collapse at 8:46 AM.' She didn't notice the virus spreading through the network.

"By 8:34, the General Manager stormed in and fired her on the spot. 'You're done!' he roared. She tried to explain—'Sir, listen, the towers will collapse in ten minutes! It's in the email!'—but he dismissed it as nonsense, blaming her for crashing the system. 'Get out!' he bellowed as she gestured helplessly at the window.

"I ran downstairs to find Dad, hoping he'd sort it out. Then—BANG!—two air-to-ground missiles and a jet slammed into the building. We were on the ground floor when nineteen terrorists, hijacking four planes, struck. The twin towers became a hellscape—screams echoing, a woman dangling from a ledge. I climbed up to help, but Mom didn't make it. I got some kids out, though, dragging them through the chaos as the fire roared and the cries grew unbearable.

"Within two hours, both towers crumbled, flattening nearby structures. Dust and debris shot a hundred meters into the air—black and blue smoke, thick with toxic fumes, choking the streets. Cars were crushed, fifty-odd bystanders suffocated in the haze. Over three thousand perished, including the hijackers. One man leapt from a plane mid-crash—I saw him, but no one else seemed to. The smoke and flames blinded everyone, and he vanished from their minds. That day broke us all, but I couldn't forget him—who was he?"

Her words hung heavy in the room. Raju exhaled softly. "I'm so sorry about your mom," he said, his sincerity palpable.

"It's alright," Alexa replied, brushing it off with practiced calm. She turned to her brother, her eyes narrowing. "Henry, did you know Emma before today?"

"No," he said, oblivious to the undercurrent in her voice.

"Alexa," Henry ventured, "why the sudden interest in Emma?"

"Because her mother died in that same disaster," she said flatly.

"She mentioned Yogi's funding her studies," Henry mused. "What's that about?"

"She's no common thief," Alexa explained. "She's at Cambridge, working for Yogi."

Henry frowned. "I'm at Cambridge too, but I've never seen her."

"You've never spotted her in class?" Raju asked, his mind tracing Yogi's web of influence.

"She's not in my classes," Henry said, shifting uncomfortably.

Alexa smirked. "That's because Henry's too busy munching popcorn outside, ogling the girls instead of attending lectures."

"Hey, cut it out!" Henry protested, a hint of defensiveness in his tone. "Last month, you promised to tell me about your new project, Sis."

"Relax," she said, unruffled. "It's just photographing historical monuments worldwide."

"That's it?" Henry raised an eyebrow. "Fine. Tomorrow, we'll both meet Emma, alright?"

Raju turned to Henry, his tone gentle but probing. "So, Henry, what's your real vice—popcorn or teenage girls?"

Henry grinned. "More than you'd guess. But it's just the popcorn, not the girls."

"Stop eating it," Raju advised. "It's laced with perfluorooctanoic acid—toxic stuff, according to recent studies."

"Got it," Henry muttered, sheepish. "Thanks for the heads-up."

Alexa and Vijay burst into laughter, the sound filling the room. "Raju's finally whipped Henry into shape," Vijay quipped, wiping a tear from his eye.

Alexa's gaze shifted to Raju, sharp and curious. "What's behind the museum robbery?" she asked.

Raju paused, the weight of her question settling over him like a storm cloud on the horizon.

6

Who is Yogi?

Alexa's voice cut through the room, sharp and urgent. "How did it come to this? The capstone, I mean." Her mind raced, piecing together the threads of the story she'd just heard. "There's a connection—between the museum robbery and that man who leapt from the jet."

"What? Who was he?" Raju asked, his tone edged with disbelief.

"Yogi," she murmured, the name falling like a stone into still water.

Raju's eyes widened. "How's that possible?"

Vijay leaned forward, his voice steady but grave. "Yes, Raju. He was one of the pilots who brought down the World Trade Center. But he's no terrorist."

"Then who is he, really?" Raju pressed, a knot of worry tightening in his chest. Questions piled up, relentless and unanswered: Why did Yogi want the capstone? Why not money? What was his endgame? The uncertainties pressed against Raju's mind, a storm threatening to break.

"Raju," Vijay said, pulling him back to the moment.

"Yes?" he replied, blinking.

"Listen closely. To understand Yogi, you need to know about his father, Vikram. He was an honest soldier, like you—disciplined, upright. We grew up together here in London, classmates through school and college. Life pulled us apart, though. I started as a jailor before turning to archaeology; Vikram joined India's Border Security Force. He never spoke of his struggles at the border—kept them locked away.

"I only met his father once, as a child. Then, a month after I started at London Central Prison, I learned he was an inmate there—a criminal, locked up for years. Vikram's father had tried to orchestrate a massive theft of Egyptian treasures."

"An archaeologist?" Raju interjected, surprise flickering across his face.

"Exactly," Vijay said, nodding. "Five years later, I was promoted to security-in-chief. Vikram returned from India with his six-year-old son, Yogi. 'My wife died giving birth to him,' he told me. 'Vijay, can you watch him for a month? Duty calls me back to the border.' I agreed, of course. He left, but he never returned. A month later, I heard he was among 3,105 prisoners held in China—captured after the Indian army crossed the Line of Control in August 1978. I kept it from Yogi, but somehow, he knew."

Vijay paused, his gaze distant. "One day, Yogi asked to visit the prison with me. 'I want to see it—the cells, the atmosphere,' he said. I warned him to behave, and we went. I left him in the office for five minutes, but when I came back, he was gone. I searched everywhere, panic rising—only to find him back in the office, calm as ever. 'Uncle Vijay, I've been looking for you!' he said. I scolded him, but he just apologized. Something shifted in him that day—sadness, envy, I couldn't tell. I suspected he'd met his grandfather, Amarnath, in there."

"Amarnath?" Raju echoed.

"A gaunt, sallow man—beak-nosed, hollow-eyed, frail but cunning. I didn't confirm it until six years later. When I asked Yogi what happened, he only said two words: 'Egypt' and 'Capstone.'"

"Capstone?" Raju frowned. "What stone?"

"'Energy,'" Vijay quoted, mimicking Yogi's nervous tone. "That's all he'd give me. I pressed, but he clammed up. I knew then—Amarnath had filled his head with tales of Egypt. That old man was a smuggler, a dangerous one. The courts sentenced him to death, and Yogi learned of it early.

"I confronted Amarnath myself. 'Why are you dragging your grandson into this nonsense?' I demanded. 'What's your goal?' His eyes glinted, wild and unrepentant. 'To rule the world with the Capstone's power,' he said. 'You're intrigued too, aren't you?' I shouted at him, furious, but he just smirked and launched into his story.

"'For thirty years, I've studied it,' he said. 'I found proof in the manuscripts of Al-Rashid, an explorer who scoured the Great Pyramid and royal tombs six centuries ago. He wrote of a capstone—a tiny, miraculous thing with boundless supernatural power. It could make humans immortal, channel cosmic energy, serve as an elixir of life. Placed in the pyramid, it would awaken the Sphinx—a living guardian obeying its master.'"

Raju's breath caught. "Is that real?"

"Amarnath believed it," Vijay said grimly. "He claimed a friend, Thomson, gave him pages from a journal proving it."

"James!" Raju exclaimed. "He mentioned that journal at the museum—vaguely, but it fits."

"Does it?" Vijay raised an eyebrow. "When Yogi turned twenty-four, he changed. He'd vanish for hours, return late, surrounded by friends I never met. He grew irritable, secretive. One night, he left without a word. The next morning, I found a letter on his bed."

Vijay's voice softened as he recited it from memory:

"'Dear Uncle Vijay, I'm sorry to write this. I'm leaving your home, your country, for India. I have an ambition to chase. Thank you for treating me like a son, for making me who I am. I won't return. Yours, Yogi.' I wept reading it. Nine years later, I tracked him down—he'd become a billionaire in India. It humbled me, but it broke my heart too."

He wiped his eyes, steadying himself. "Raju, Yogi's after the Capstone and Egypt's treasures. We have to stop him."

"Don't worry, Mr. Vijay," Raju said, a spark of resolve in his voice. "I've got a plan. We'll stop him soon."

"What plan?" Vijay asked, intrigued.

Raju grinned faintly. "We'll rob the robbers."

7

Robbers are robbed

Raju's resolve crystallized into a singular purpose: Yogi would face him, and with Vijay's aid, retribution would be exacted. The sting of betrayal fueled his every thought.

"Raju, what's this plan of yours?" Alexa asked, her voice laced with hesitant curiosity.

"Hold on, Alexa," Raju replied, a spark of anticipation in his tone. "Mr. Vijay, I need your team assembled. Then I'll unveil it." His words carried a quiet thrill, a strategist poised to strike.

"Very well," Vijay said, a nod sealing his agreement. "You've got my support."

The team convened in a vast, echoing chamber— forty-three souls ready to be molded. Raju snatched a crisp sheet from Vijay's desk, his grip firm. "We're going to Egypt," he declared, his eyes sweeping the assembly like a general rallying his troops.

"Who's 'we'?" Alexa pressed, her question hanging in the air.

"The team," Raju said sharply. "Not you, Henry, or Mr. Vijay."

Turning to Vijay, he asked, "Who's your sharpest leader? I need the best."

"Johnny," Vijay answered, gesturing to a lean, hawk-eyed man. "He commands our top fifteen."

"Johnny!" Vijay summoned. The man stepped forward, and together with Raju and the elite squad, they crafted a scheme to topple Yogi's empire. Raju pulled a brittle parchment from his battered suitcase.

"A map?" a voice ventured from the ranks.

"To the King's Chamber," Raju confirmed. "Lifted from James' office."

"What's the play?" Johnny asked, his gaze locked on the map with predatory focus.

"We cripple Yogi's core—his artifact smuggling," Raju said, his voice a blade slicing through doubt. "Egypt's his lifeline. We block his crew from plundering the pyramids and the Valley of the Kings."

"You're right," Vijay murmured, his stare piercing the distance. "That's his profit engine. But how? One misstep, and we're sunk for years."

"Could be," Raju admitted. "So we bind ourselves first." He brandished the paper. "Sign this pact. If Yogi turns anyone and they derail us, they'll pay dearly. No room for weakness—commit or step back." His tone was stern, a commander brooking no dissent.

The team buzzed with fervor, signatures flowing freely. At first light, they set out for Egypt.

Four hours later, they landed in Cairo, then rolled into Giza by bus. They bunked in a hotel, the desert night's chill seeping into their bones. Raju wrestled with humility and rage, Yogi's treachery a relentless specter as his team slept.

He rose before dawn, pounding on doors to rouse them. As he knocked, a voice—silken yet sinister—slithered from behind. "Morning, Mr. Raju."

Raju whirled, stunned. The team was already up, primed to move. "Did you sleep well?" Johnny asked, his grin sly.

"Well enough," Raju fibbed, meeting Johnny's steady look. "Let's move."

"Where?" Johnny replied.

"Great Pyramid, then the Valley—post-breakfast," Raju said.

"Your call," Johnny conceded, a flicker of scrutiny in his eyes. "Downstairs, then."

They dug into ful medames—spiced fava beans, hearty and warm—before sailing the Nile on a felucca, its sails billowing like wings. At Giza, Raju drank in the pyramids: Khufu's grandeur, Khafre's limestone crown, Menkaure's quiet might. Built for Ra's glory in the Fifth Dynasty, their granite skins glowed with ancient secrets. Awe tugged at him, briefly softening his edge.

Tourists swarmed in as the morning wore on. "Raju!" Johnny's shout cut through the din.

"Yeah?" Raju turned. "Drop the 'Mr.'—just Raju."

"Got it. We need to get inside before they lock up, right?" Johnny said, scanning the throng.

"Exactly," Raju agreed. "We're tourists—blend in, stay safe."

"Tourists, not troublemakers," Roger muttered, smirking.

"Zip it!" Johnny growled, his patience thin.

"Johnny, can you decipher the old script?" Raju asked.

"Hieroglyphs? I'm your man," Johnny said with a quick nod.

"Smart moves only," Raju warned.

By midday, the heat soared to 48 degrees, scattering the crowd. Raju's team darted into the Great Pyramid an hour before closing, threading the Grand Gallery and scaling the Great Step. The King's Chamber loomed— red granite walls etched with faded tales, a cool floor cradling a fractured sarcophagus at its heart.

Three hours ticked by in silence, then footsteps clattered from the entrance. The team melted into the basement's shadows. A rat's shrill squeak pierced the quiet near Rahim. "Someone's here," a rough voice rasped.

"Quiet, idiot!" another snapped.

Raju peered up, sweat cascading down his brow, his team taut with unease. The murmurs closed in. He and Johnny tucked into a shadowed crevice beneath the slick floor, cloaked in darkness.

"Yogi's guards," Johnny hissed, eyes on the entryway.

A granite platform loomed five feet above, its entrance flanked by a tight passage. Raju and Johnny pressed into the gaps on either side, the space swelling like a shallow den. Tension coiled in Raju's chest, sharp and electric.

Eleven guards stormed in. One vaulted the slick floor, slipped, and crashed into the gap with a shout. The rest swarmed the chamber, chiseling at the ceiling toward a sealed realm. "Help me!" the fallen guard cried.

Raju's instincts flared—they sought a hidden chamber, untouched by time. He pounced, gagging the man with a iron grip. The guard flailed, muffled gasps leaking out, alerting the others. They charged. Raju snapped the man's neck and dropped him with a fist.

The guards leapt down, guns gleaming. Raju surged, hoisting the dead man as a shield and hurling him into a shooter. The bullet meant for Raju ripped through the corpse instead, blood pooling fast.

His team clashed with the guards, a savage dance of fists and fury. Raju's kick sent one skull-first into the wall, a sickening crunch echoing. Torches spun to the floor, their light skittering across the glassy surface, blinding in its glare. "Can't see them!" Johnny snarled, grappling in the fray.

"Torches up—hold steady!" Raju ordered.

His heart slammed like a forge as a guard's punch doubled him over. He recoiled, then leapt, a high kick felling the man with a wail. Two guards chased Johnny, but he ricocheted off the wall, crashing down on them, their heads splitting on impact.

"Raju, watch out!" Johnny yelled. Raju ducked a swinging leg, seizing it and yanking the guard off balance. A guttural curse rumbled from the dark. Raju spun—too late. A shot rang out, and Johnny crumpled, a bullet from Rahim, their own, buried in his skull.

"No!" Raju bellowed, his laser pistol flashing to life. Beams cut down one guard, maimed another. The rest bolted, fleeing the lethal storm. Twenty bodies—ally and enemy—littered the chamber when silence fell.

Raju slipped away an hour later, summoning the police. Roger's footage, a grim miracle, exposed the ruse. Yogi's impostors were cuffed, new guards installed, but Johnny's loss carved a hollow in Raju's gut. The police pressed the captives, but they gave nothing—not even Yogi's name—leaving the mastermind's shadow untouched, a riddle yet to unravel.

8

I lost my income

Eleven men were hauled into custody, their wrists bound by the clink of handcuffs. Raju filed a criminal charge against Rahim, the traitor who'd gunned down Johnny, and spun a web of suspicion. He laid bare his suspicions of Yogi's shadowy machinations. Yet Yogi was a phantom— meticulous, elusive—leaving the police grasping at smoke. With no concrete evidence, the court absolved him, a bitter pill Raju couldn't swallow.

Disillusioned, Raju grew wary, convinced Yogi's tendrils snaked through the police force. He strode into the office of Cairo's new commissioner—a grizzled man of sixty, freshly transferred—and demanded a purge. "Verify every officer's background before they guard the monuments," he urged.

"Absolutely," the commissioner replied, his grin a jagged slash across his face. Raju, buoyed by the promise, left the room—only to pause at the door, ears pricking to a hushed exchange.

"Sir, I've got doubts about Raju," the head constable murmured.

"What's that?" the commissioner snapped.

"He's got evidence—Yogi could be nabbed soon," the constable ventured.

"Quiet!" the commissioner barked, eyes darting to his boots. "I fed Raju a lie. You and I—we're Yogi's men. We toil for him, our master. That's the game."

A roar erupted from behind the door. "Oh, he's your master, is he?"

"Who's there?" the commissioner bellowed.

"Me," Raju said, stepping in with thunder in his voice. He snatched his phone from the desk—a covert plant—and brandished it. "Your confession's recorded. I'll hand this to the high court. You're finished."

The commissioner's hand twitched toward his revolver, but Raju was lightning. A swift kick sent the gun skittering across the floor. "Don't even think about it. I know your mind."

"No, please—not the court!" the commissioner pleaded, hands quaking.

"Then list every Yogi loyalist in your ranks," Raju demanded. "Or else."

"Don't!" the commissioner stammered. "I'll do it, sir."

"Four days," Raju warned. "And not a word to Yogi. Clear?"

His phone chirped mid-standoff. He answered, unflinching.

"Raju, where are you?" Alexa's voice sang through the line, bright and lilting.

"Cairo, commissioner's office," he replied. "Yesterday felt like a setup, but we're still in control."

"That's great," she said. "Busy? I'll ring later."

"Yeah, bye," he said, smooth as silk, then turned back to the commissioner. "I've known you a day, but you reek of fraud."

"What?" the man sputtered, dazed.

"Why's Yogi planting men everywhere?" Raju pressed, anger flaring.

"I won't betray my master," the commissioner shot back.

"Fine." Raju stormed out, only to double back moments later. "Forgot my phone," he said, snagging it from the desk before vanishing again.

The commissioner froze, hands trembling anew. "He recorded us again," the constable whispered. With a gasp, the man toppled backward, unconscious.

Raju dialed Alexa. "I'm done here. I'll be back tomorrow."

"Great! Uncle Vijay wants a word," she chirped.

"Tell him Yogi's days are numbered. Flight's at five," Raju said, boarding swiftly.

In London, he delivered the recordings to the police, who bore them to the high court. The evidence—ironclad from the first witness—sparked a global inquisition into police and security ranks. Within four days, Yogi's puppets surrendered, their networks crumbling. Yet none named their master.

Yogi vanished, a wraith retreating to Britain's underbelly, his empire stalled. Fear gnawed at him now—Raju had to be checked.

A month later, in his shadowed lair, Yogi's wrath erupted. "I lost my income!" he roared.

"Sir, don't despair," his assistant soothed. "Call your ally in London—Pharaoh. Sharper than a blade, he'll gut Raju with his own hand."

"Yes," Yogi snarled, eyes glinting. "Pharaoh's my dagger. Raju won't see it coming."

9

The only way to stop 'Him'

Dawn broke over northern England's highland road, a serpentine ribbon threading east to west along the coast. The air was crisp, spring's chill lingering as the sun breached the sea's horizon, a molten infant casting golden rays across the unprotected twists of the path. Flanked by mountain slopes, their peaks wreathed in mist and kissed by verdant bounty, the scene was a painter's dream—save for the absence of guardrails, a silent dare to the unwary.

Two trucks lumbered along this perilous stretch, fresh from the shipyard. One brimmed with illicit sandalwood, smuggled from Southeast Asia; the other, a white container, bore secrets yet unseen. Behind them, a black motorcycle roared, its tires clawing the asphalt with ferocious grip. The rider—Pharaoh—was a force incarnate: blond, copper-black hair swept back, clad in a hooded jacket, his presence as unyielding as the cliffs. A decorated officer, he drew his revolver from his vest and fired, the bullet tearing through the container's chained lock. The doors burst open, and Pharaoh's breath caught.

A cascade of luxury cars spilled forth—three BMWs, black and silver, tumbling into chaos. One rolled wildly, nearly clipping him; another flipped over it, landing upright with a thud. Pharaoh braked hard, his bike rearing onto its front wheel. He vaulted off, airborne, crashing into a car's side mirror. Glass shattered as he hit the road with a guttural "AAAh!" Pain seared through him, but the third car barreled down, exploding in a fireball that sprayed mirror shards like deadly confetti.

Teetering at the road's unguarded edge, Pharaoh rolled east, clutching the brink to halt his fall. With a grunt, he hauled himself up, sprinting to his bike sprawled on the pavement. He mounted it, the engine snarling to life, back tire spinning dust into a gritty cloud. Accelerating with relentless fury, he chased the fleeing trucks, closing the gap. With a final surge, he leapt from his bike onto the container's doorstep, the motorcycle flipping and bursting into flames behind him.

Scrambling atop the container, he eyed the lead truck just ahead. He darted forward, leaping to its cabin as a burly figure emerged. "Pharaoh, what're you doing? Get lost—or I'll end you!" the man bellowed.

"Doing my job," Pharaoh shot back, perched atop the sandalwood stack.

The man raised a revolver, but Pharaoh was a blur—dodging, unslinging a double-barreled rifle from his back. He swung into the air, evading the shot, and fired twice. One bullet felled the gunman; the second pierced the driver. Both slumped, lifeless, as the trucks collided in a thunderous crunch.

Pharaoh launched skyward, sandalwood splinters pelting his back. A minute earlier, he'd planted a time bomb in the container—now it detonated, a maelstrom of smoke and flame swallowing the wreckage. He'd leapt from the cliff just in time, plummeting before his parachute bloomed, guiding him gently to the seashore. The explosion's debris rained harmlessly behind him, and he touched down, victorious—smugglers thwarted.

Three hours later, he boarded a train to London. Mid-journey, his phone buzzed. Yogi's voice crackled through, taut with panic. "Pharaoh, I'm in deep trouble!"

"What's wrong?" Pharaoh asked, sensing the dread beneath Yogi's words.

"Come quick—I'm in Liverpool, holed up in my hideout. I'll send details. We've got a problem—he's found a way to stop me. I need you!" Yogi's tone was a dull, furious rasp, desperation bleeding through.

Pharaoh's jaw tightened. The hunt was far from over.

10

The Revenge

At that precise moment, Yogi dispatched an MMS to Pharaoh's phone, embedding a photograph of Raju along with his particulars. Accompanying the image was a terse message:

Don't let him slip away—he's far too dangerous! He's inflicted severe damage on my revenue. Begin the hunt immediately. My men are already on his trail. Meet me this evening....

Pharaoh absorbed the directive and set off toward Parliament Road.

Simultaneously, a relentless downpour drenched the city, cloaking the sky in a shroud of moisture. Visibility dwindled as the rain blurred the streets. Raju and Henry found themselves ensnared in a snarl of traffic at the four-way junction where Westminster Bridge met Parliament Square. The gridlock, worsened by the collision of an oil tanker, was paralyzing. Abandoning their motorcycle near a telephone booth opposite a shopping plaza, they sought refuge beneath a footpath shelter.

"What a mess!" Henry exclaimed, wiping rain from his brow. "The road's a haze, isn't it?"

"Still better than dealing with Yogi," Raju quipped dryly.

Henry grinned. "Remember how I got your wallet back from that girl?"

"Yeah, Alexa bailed you out," Raju muttered. "What's that supposed to mean?"

"I promised my sister I'd take her to see Emma," Henry said, glancing at the sodden sky. "But this rain's ruined that plan."

"Where's Alexa now?" Raju asked, his tone softening.

"Probably Charing Cross Road," Henry replied. "She's got a thing for those dusty bookstores—piles of obscure history tomes."

Raju's eyes narrowed. "No, she's trying to save you again."

"What are you on about?" Henry whispered, suddenly alert.

"I suspect she's gone to meet Emma," Raju said, his voice tinged with dread. "This isn't the time for it."

Henry fumbled with his phone, dialing Alexa's number. "Her phone's off—still. That's not like her."

Raju's intuition proved grimly accurate. Alexa, at that very moment, was steering her white sedan through the storm, having paused to snap photographs of the London Eye and Tower Bridge. The river Thames churned beneath the raised spans of the bridge, swollen by the deluge. Her car now idled at the edge of a squalid alley—the same one where she'd once rescued Henry from the vicious gang. Stepping out, she unfurled a green floral umbrella, her burgundy jeans and sleeveless sea-green crop top stark against the gloom. Raindrops glittered like diamonds as they struck the canopy, the sky roaring with thunder.

Halfway down the muddy path, Alexa paused, her striking features glistening with stray droplets. A sharp DHUBB!—the sound of someone striking a water barrel—pierced the air. She whipped around, curiosity flickering in her eyes.

"HELP ME! SOMEBODY, PLEASE!" a shrill, feminine voice cried out from the same direction.

"Emma? Is that you?" Alexa shouted, already moving. "I'm coming!"

"ALEXA, HELP!" the voice wailed, desperate and insistent.

She sprinted toward the sound, water splashing beneath her boots. Rounding a corner, her foot caught on a submerged metal pipe. She stumbled, crashing into the muddy deluge, her clothes now streaked with grime. Scrambling upright, she froze—seven towering figures loomed before her, closing in. With a swift kick, she felled two, then bolted forward.

A chilling laugh sliced through the chaos. Alexa spun to see Emma perched on a rickety armchair, her expression unhinged. "Caught you at last," Emma sneered. "We thought your brother would stumble into our trap, but looks like we've netted a bigger prize."

"How dare you target me—and Henry?" Alexa spat, her voice trembling with fury.

"No time to waste, boys," Emma barked. "Get it done."

Rage flared across Alexa's face, her cheeks flushing crimson as she clenched her teeth. She lunged at Emma, leaping into the air—but mid-flight, a tranquilizer dart struck her. Her body slackened, and she crashed into the chair, toppling it as Emma sidestepped with a smirk. Alexa crumpled to the ground, unconscious.

"She'll be out for three hours," Narendra remarked coolly, eyeing her sprawled form. Emma and her crew had succeeded—not in capturing Henry, but in seizing Alexa. They spirited her away to a clandestine hideout, shrouded in secrecy.

Ten minutes later, oblivious to Alexa's fate, Raju and Henry lingered at the traffic jam. "An hour already," Raju grumbled. "What's taking so long?"

"It's clearing up," Henry noted, peering at the road. "Should we move?"

"Not yet," Raju cautioned. "Patience."

"Raju," Henry murmured, "I think someone's watching us—from across the lane."

Raju followed his gaze. "You're right."

A silver Benz idled just behind them, innocuous amid the chaos. Across the road, Pharaoh sat trapped in the same snarl, riding in a cab. For an hour, he'd studied Raju and Henry. Now, he emerged, clambering onto the hood of a car ahead of him. With agility born of purpose, he vaulted from vehicle to vehicle, closing the distance. Drawing a hefty pistol from his coat, he took aim as Raju and Henry conversed, unaware.

Two shots rang out as Pharaoh leaped. "Raju!" Henry yelled, yanking him down. The bullets sliced through the rain, missing their mark and slamming into the Benz's fuel tank. Pharaoh landed in a roll and vanished into the melee.

A deafening BANG! erupted as the car exploded, hurling shards of glass, burning rubber, and bodies into the air. Vibrations rippled through the street as panic seized the crowd. Raju and Henry darted to safety, the downpour and swift-acting firefighters curbing the blaze's spread.

"My God," Henry breathed, stunned. "The rain saved us."

"Four dead, I'd guess," Raju said grimly.

"Someone's after you," Henry insisted. "They aimed for you."

"No surprise there," Raju replied. "That Benz—I saw it ten days ago."

"Where?"

"Yogi's villa."

"So those bodies… Yogi's men?"

"Exactly," Raju confirmed. "We need to get out of here—now."

11

'He' is trying to kill you!

The rain finally relented, its drumming ceasing as Raju and Henry arrived home. They shed their sodden clothes, toweling their hair dry in a quiet, shared relief.

"Shall we head to lunch?" Raju asked, breaking the silence. "Mr. Vijay might be waiting."

"Yeah," Henry replied with a faint grin, though unease gnawed at him. "At least we're out of danger now."

"No, Henry," Raju countered, his voice grave. "The danger's only just begun. We need to escape these deadly games."

Henry glanced at his watch. "It's past noon. Uncle Vijay mentioned Alexa hasn't come home for lunch." He peered out the window, scanning the empty street.

"What? She's not back?" Raju's tone sharpened with concern.

"Don't worry," Henry said, forcing calm. "She's probably tied up with work. Let's just go eat."

Before Raju could respond, his phone buzzed insistently. He answered, wary. "Hello?"

"Hi, Raju. How's your day treating you?" came a smooth, taunting voice.

Raju's jaw tightened. "What's this about, Yogi? Another one of your games?"

"Precisely," Yogi purred. "Put Alexa's brother on."

"How do you know Alexa?" Raju demanded, fury rising.

"Because I've got her," Yogi replied coolly. "Kidnapped, to be exact."

"Is this some sick joke?" Raju snarled. "How dare you?"

"Oh, it's true," Yogi said. "And you'll do as I say."

"What are you blabbering about?" Raju's voice was rough with worry.

"The capstone," Yogi said, chuckling darkly. "That's what I'm after."

"Raju, what's he saying?" Henry interjected, leaning closer. "Where's Alexa?"

"Listen carefully, Raju," Yogi continued. "Bring me the capstone, and I'll let her go. Cross me, and she's dead. You've got two days—get it from the British Museum before the clock runs out." Sweat beaded on Raju's brow as Yogi hung up.

"Raju, what's happened to Alexa?" Henry's voice broke, tears brimming.

"Yogi's taken her," Raju admitted, his nerves fraying.

"Why?" Henry sobbed. "I thought Emma's gang grabbed her. What do they want?"

"It's me they're after," Raju said bitterly. "I won't let anyone suffer because of me."

"It's not your fault," Henry insisted.

"If he harms her, I'll end him," Raju roared, hurling his phone to the floor with a crack.

Henry's cries echoed through the room. "Don't worry," Raju said, softening. "I'll save her. But it'll take two days."

"Not you alone," Henry whispered. "We should go to the police."

"Yogi's holed up somewhere clever," Raju replied. "A police move could spook him."

"What's he demanding?" Henry pressed.

"The crystal capstone from the Natural History Museum," Raju said. "Two days to steal it and trade it for Alexa."

"And the attempt on your life?"

"Not Yogi," Raju reasoned. "He needs me alive for this. His men died too—someone else is hunting us both."

"Pharaoh," Henry muttered. "Only he could pull that off. I've seen him twice. Alexa knows him."

"What?"

"I don't know details—ask her when we get her back," Henry said, shaking his head.

"I'll save her regardless," Raju vowed.

"You're going to Yogi's lair?"

"No," Raju said sharply. "I'm hitting the museum for that capstone."

"Raju, that's insane—suicide!" Henry warned. "Yogi wants you locked up. Let the police handle it."

"You think I'd abandon Alexa?" Raju shot back. "Yogi's a man of his word—ruthlessly so. I've seen it. This is my only shot."

"Fine," Henry relented. "But be careful. The museum's beefed up security—new staff, tight measures."

"That's why Yogi needs me," Raju said grimly. "Should we see Mr. Vijay?"

"Good call," Henry agreed. "He might help."

They left the room, ascending the stairs past a gallery of family portraits. They entered the circular meeting hall—granite-floored, its pink walls adorned with elegant wooden carvings and glittering chandeliers. Tension clung to them as they entered.

Vijay lounged in a cushioned black armchair, conversing with his men. "There you are," he said, glancing up. "Sit."

Raju and Henry settled onto a sofa opposite him. "We need to speak privately," Henry said, eyeing the five men scattered around.

"Alright—Simon, Stewart, George, you lot, step outside. I'll call you back," Vijay ordered. The room cleared, leaving just the three of them.

"What's this about, Henry?" Vijay asked, his tone gentle.

"Alexa," Henry replied, head bowed, voice trembling.

"What's happened?" Vijay pressed, noting their unease.

"She's been kidnapped by Yogi," Henry confessed.

"What do you mean—she kidnapped him, or the other way around?"

"It's true, Mr. Vijay," Raju interjected, then recounted the call, his suspicions coming out in a rush.

Vijay leaned forward, his expression darkening as the weight of their words settled in.

12

Henry's fury

After their conversation, Henry's disappointment in Emma deepened. Her deception—making him believe she'd kidnapped Alexa—shattered the trust he'd once placed in her. Determined to confront her, Henry strode down the corridor, yanked his phone from his back pocket, and dialed the number Emma had given him ten days earlier. He pressed the device to his ear, his voice tight with urgency.

"Emma, it's Henry! Can you hear me?"

"Always, my friend!" came her cheerful reply. "How are you and your sister?"

"Where's Alexa?" he demanded, his anger simmering as he spoke each word deliberately.

Emma laughed lightly. "Oh, Henry, how could you think we'd taken her?"

"You're a sly one!" he roared, his voice echoing across the fourth-floor balcony where he stood. "What do you want?"

"It's not for me—it's for him," she said, pausing mysteriously.

"What are you talking about?"

"He wants you, your sister, and Raju. We've already got her," Emma replied, her tone brimming with glee. "Henry, I need to tell you something important. Can you meet me?"

"Where are you?"

"The usual spot," she said calmly.

"Are you messing with me again?" Henry pressed, sweat beading on his forehead. "Where's Alexa?"

"No games this time," Emma insisted. "Same time, same place." With that, she hung up.

"Damn it!" Henry yelled, his hope crumbling. He stood there, lost in frustration, until Raju rushed toward him.

"What's wrong, Henry?" Raju asked, concern etched on his face. "What did she say?"

"That treacherous girl!" Henry growled. "She wants us to go to her."

"Why?"

"I don't know!" Henry snapped, his nerves fraying. "She said someone wants all of us."

"Either way," Raju said, his voice steady, "we need to proceed with caution."

Henry's mind churned with worry for Alexa and disbelief at Emma's betrayal. He'd once considered her his closest friend, but now he resolved to face her—with

Raju by his side. That night, sleep eluded him. Sitting on his twin bed in the dim attic, he stared at a photo of Alexa—perched on a cane chair in a red hooded jacket and gray jeans, her smile radiant. Tears streamed from his blue eyes as he wept loudly into the silence. Hours dragged by, and a feverish exhaustion settled over him. By dawn, his only comfort was the trust he placed in Raju.

As sunlight crept into the corridor, Henry marched forward, a faint smirk tugging at his lips despite his nerves. Raju appeared beside him.

"Morning, Raju," Henry said, his voice shaky but warm.

"Morning," Raju replied, reading the strain in Henry's face. "Didn't sleep, did you?"

"I did," Henry lied.

"Tonight, I'll save your sister," Raju declared firmly. "I promise."

"Raju," Henry stammered, "can I ask you something?"

"Of course."

"Why risk so much for Alexa against Yogi?"

Raju's gaze softened. "Because I see you all as my family. After years alone, I finally have people I care about."

"What does Yogi want with that stone?" Henry asked, curiosity piqued.

"He seeks immortality," Raju explained. "He's trapped in Maaya."

"Maaya?" Henry frowned. "His wife? Some tech program?"

"No," Raju chuckled. "Maaya is delusion—an illusion that lures people into ruthless pursuits. It's everywhere, especially for someone young like you, disguised as desire. Yogi's caught in its grip."

"Fascinating," Henry murmured. "Can I come with you, Raju?"

"It's too dangerous," Raju warned.

"I won't be a burden," Henry pleaded.

"No, stay back," Raju insisted firmly.

"Alright," Henry relented, voice trembling. "Good luck."

Though desperate to save Alexa, Henry was sidelined by Raju's refusal. He gazed out at the rain-soaked lawns, disappointment gnawing at him. Raju, understanding the ache of losing family, felt a kinship with Henry despite their differences. He glanced at the empty driveway—no cars in sight to take him to the museum for reconnaissance. Heading to the meeting hall, he approached Mr. Vijay.

"Can I borrow your car?" Raju asked.

"Of course," Vijay replied. "Hold on, I'll call George to bring the keys. He's probably driving it up from the garage now." Moments later, George arrived and handed the keys to Raju.

Raju dashed to the car and slid into the driver's seat. A soft thud came from behind him. Whipping around, he found Henry in the backseat, grinning sheepishly.

"Henry!" Raju exclaimed, half-amused, half-exasperated. "Fine, I'm heading to the museum. You're with me now."

"I want to see it too," Henry said, his tone earnest. "Please."

"Alright," Raju agreed. "But we act like regular visitors."

"Got it," Henry whispered.

Raju's apprehension doubled with Henry along, but he steeled himself. Starting the engine, he guided the car onto the slick road, determined to move carefully.

13

On the happening

As they cruised along the 29 Barrier Point Road, the car paused at an ancient beacon near the midpoint to the British Museum, just past Tower Bridge.

"Raju, can you stop here?" Henry asked politely.

Raju pulled over abruptly onto the left side of the road, next to a muddy lane. "Why now, Henry? Is something urgent?" he asked, glancing at Tower Bridge in the rearview mirror. It was midday, yet rain fell steadily, leaving the road eerily empty.

"Emma told me to meet her here," Henry replied.

"You said she kidnapped Alexa," Raju said gently. "Are you sure about this?"

"Yes," Henry insisted, "but I think she's trying to tell us something."

"No, Henry, this could be a trap to grab you too," Raju warned. He stepped out of the car, shutting the door quickly. "Don't worry—I'm here for you."

"Anyway, I'll introduce you to her," Henry said, climbing out. "Come on, let's go. She's honest—she doesn't lie."

"Alright, Henry," Raju said, his tone heavy with duty. "We'll see what she has to say."

Leaving the car behind, they trudged twenty yards down the muddy street.

"Wait," Henry said, glancing back at the vehicle. "I left my phone in there." He turned and took two steps toward it.

BANG!

In an instant, the car erupted in a deafening explosion, flames licking the air as charred debris scattered. The front tire, engulfed in smoldering fire, hurtled toward them, narrowly missing before splashing into a puddle on their right.

"Henry!" Raju shouted, yanking him back. The blast's force threw them several yards, but they landed with only minor scrapes.

"That was horrific!" Henry gasped, staring at the wreckage.

"Police are here," Raju said tensely, looking skyward as a helicopter descended. Six officers emerged, inspecting the scene, trying to pinpoint the cause of the car bomb. The vehicle was now a mangled heap, unrecognizable.

"Let's get out of here," Raju muttered, his gaze dark.

"What?" Henry stammered.

"It's a waste of time—we don't need this mess," Raju replied.

They slipped away before the police could question them, heading deeper into the muddy street to find Emma.

"Emma!" Henry bellowed. A gentle tap landed on his shoulder. He spun around.

"Shh," Emma hushed him, a finger to her lips.

"There you are!" Henry growled, grabbing her arm and shoving it away. She turned to Raju.

"You're Raju, I assume?" she asked, eyeing him curiously.

"Yes," Raju replied sharply.

"Where's Alexa?" Henry demanded, his anger flaring as he glared at her.

"She's safe, but…" Emma trailed off.

"But what?" Raju pressed, studying her face.

"I'll explain everything," she said nervously, "but not here. Follow me." She led them down a side path. Henry and Raju trailed behind.

They arrived at a construction site and entered the ground floor of a new six-story building. The corridor was pristine—sky-blue walls, marble floors—with four light-colored stools around a russet table near the drawing room. Emma arranged three stools in a circle.

"Sit," she said, her voice tight with anxiety. Fear clouded her expression.

"Where is she?" Raju asked calmly.

"She's been sent on a mission," Emma replied slowly.

"Where?" Henry snapped.

"I don't know, but she's safe," she said quickly, brushing her hair back from her face.

"You're lying again!" Henry shouted, leaping from his stool.

"I get how you feel, Henry," Emma said evenly. "Please, just hear me out. I'm not with Yogi's crew."

"Then who are you?" Henry demanded.

"I'm James Thomson's only daughter," she revealed.

A stunned silence filled the room. Henry and Raju exchanged bewildered glances at her shocking admission.

"What?" Henry muttered to himself, shaken. "Why didn't Uncle Vijay ever mention this?"

"Emma, why didn't you stop the kidnapping?" Raju asked, peering at her.

"Fear," she admitted, sweat glistening on her face.

"Where's your father?" Raju pressed.

"Yogi's holding him somewhere. My brother's been missing since yesterday too," she said, her voice trembling. "Yogi forced me into this. That's why I need you—you're the only one who can stand up to him."

"Why didn't you tell us sooner?" Raju asked.

"It happened too fast—Yogi planned it all so precisely," she said, fidgeting.

"Someone just tried to kill us with a car bomb," Henry interjected, his voice taut.

"How?" Emma asked, startled.

"We don't know who rigged it," Henry replied.

"Anyway, I owe Henry thanks," Raju said. "Stopping to meet you saved me."

"Glad you're okay," Henry said, rubbing his nose.

"We trust you, Emma," Raju assured her. "Stay safe."

"Will you stick with us?" Henry asked.

"Of course," she nodded.

"Want to come to the British Museum?" Raju offered.

"Sure," Emma agreed. "I haven't been there in three months—not since Dad stopped working as security chief. I used to skip school to hang out there."

"Let's go then," Raju said, rising. "It's not safe here—I sense trouble."

He'd spotted a distant figure aiming a weapon their way. Warning Henry and Emma to take cover, he was stunned when Emma slipped him a revolver from her coat. Henry gaped as Raju expertly handled it. As Emma pulled Henry to safety, seven armed men stormed in. Raju fought back with deft skill, but one thug fired a rocket launcher, shattering the ground floor in a fiery BOOM! Dust and ash rained down.

Raju, Henry, and Emma narrowly escaped. Raju took down the launcher-wielding attacker with a single shot.

"What the hell was that? Who were those bastards?" Emma gasped, clutching Raju's arm in terror.

"Yogi's men," he replied grimly. "They're after you."

"Let's move!" Henry urged, darting ahead.

They caught a local train to St. Montagu Street, en route to the Natural History Museum. Fifteen minutes later, they stood in the courtyard of the British Museum. Henry gazed at Great Russell Street, while Emma and Raju admired the Indian garden out front.

"What first?" Emma asked.

"King's Library, then the art gallery," Henry suggested. "After that, the Egyptian rooms—mummies included."

"Enough, Henry," Emma teased. "I know this place better than you."

"Raju, where's the capstone?" Henry asked.

"What kind is it?" Emma added, intrigued.

"I'll explain later," Raju said. "We're headed to Room 4—Egyptian Sculpture."

"Sweet!" Henry cheered.

In Room 4, they marveled at ancient treasures. Henry gawked at the Rosetta Stone—its Egyptian hieroglyphs, Demotic script, and Greek text stacked in tiers. Emma's eyes locked onto a papyrus depicting a journey to the afterlife: Nakht, an astronomer, with Thoth, paddling across the Lake of Offerings, worshipping a heron, and Osiris's snake-headed boat gliding below.

"Stunning, right?" Emma murmured, transfixed.

"Absolutely," Henry agreed, awed.

"Come on, you two," Raju said, moving ahead. "There's more."

In the ornament gallery, Henry admired the intricate displays.

"Where's the capstone?" Emma asked.

"This way," Raju said briskly.

They entered an oblong hall in the north block, lined with ancient Egyptian spears and hammers, a vibrant carpet stretching across the floor. The room was silent, empty.

"Know any guards here, Raju?" Emma whispered.

"Nope," he replied.

"No visitors—strange," Henry noted, scanning the space.

"Most don't know about the stone. No public access either," Raju said. "Good for us—I've got VIP passes."

They approached a large shelf in the rose-colored room, its checkered ceiling aglow with chandeliers. Dim light illuminated a bulletproof case holding the capstone—a tiny marvel etched with microscopic Sanskrit and Egyptian symbols.

"Incredible," Henry breathed, staring.

"It's priceless," Raju said gravely. "Full of mystic power."

"Raju," Emma began.

"Yes?"

"I bet Yogi's after this," she said, suspicious.

"Spot on," Raju confirmed, eyes on the stone.

"Seems straightforward," Henry mused.

"Not quite," Raju countered, hand slipping into his pocket. "This is tricky."

"What are you two on about?" Emma asked Henry.

"For Alexa," he whispered.

"What?"

"Yogi wants this capstone," Henry explained, excitement flickering in his eyes. "He's forcing Raju to deliver it tonight to free her."

"So Raju has no choice," Emma said. "Is that wrong?"

"No," Raju answered firmly. "Saving an innocent girl outweighs preserving a relic. It's the key to getting Alexa back."

"It's almost evening," Emma noted, glancing at her watch.

"Time to go?" Raju asked. "I've got work after this."

"Yeah," Henry said, heading for the exit.

14

You are not alone!

Exiting Room 4, they gathered in the main hall.

"Henry, take Emma to your place—she'll be safe there," Raju instructed. "Don't stay out too late. I'll join you by early morning."

"Sounds good," Henry replied, pulling Raju into a warm hug. "You're a good man. I can't thank you enough for risking everything to save Alexa."

Henry and Emma left the museum and soon arrived at Vijay's Villa. Raju felt a wave of relief when Henry called to confirm they'd made it home safely. With half an hour until closing, Raju slipped back into the museum, blending in as a visitor. He headed for the Egyptian section, searching for a spot to evade security. The toilets—ten in a row—seemed the perfect hideout. He darted into the eighth stall.

Outside, the sun dipped below the city skyline along Great Russell Street. Guards began their rounds, sweeping through the museum. One approached the north block, entering the toilets and checking each stall. He opened the sixth—empty. The seventh—clear. As he reached for the eighth, where Raju hid, a voice boomed from afar.

"William!"

"Yes, sir!" the guard called back, abandoning his task and rushing toward the main hall. Raju exhaled—safe for now. He emerged and returned to the oblong hall housing the capstone. The room was dim, save for the faint glow illuminating the stone's case beneath a chandelier.

What's going on here? Raju wondered, stepping inside. Guards everywhere, yet this room's unprotected. Magic? Or Yogi's doing?

He crept toward the case. Suddenly, the lights flared on, and the door locked with a click. Footsteps echoed closer. Unfazed, Raju pulled a small laser cutter from his shoe's sole, tracing a twelve-inch circle in the glass. He reached in and grasped the stone.

"It's not crystal," he muttered, confused. "How? Who swapped the original?"

"It's possible," a playful male voice answered from behind.

"Who's there?" Raju shouted, spinning around.

Silence. The door burst open, and three guards charged in. Raju sprang up, kicking one down. The other two shoved him back, his hand scraping painfully against the glass. He hit the floor, and they pummeled him mercilessly.

"I'll save you, Raju," the voice whispered.

Dazed, Raju glanced over and saw a figure—Pharaoh—fighting off the guards. Before he could process it, darkness claimed him.

Pharaoh, a master of meditation and martial arts, handled crises with ease. When a guard swung at his legs, he levitated briefly, his aura shielding him, then struck the man's head and landed gracefully. In seconds, he dispatched all three.

Raju awoke, dressed in fresh robes, lying in a bedroom at Vijay's Villa. His watch read 7:30 a.m.

"Raju, you okay?" Henry asked, eyeing him oddly. "When did you get here?"

"No idea," Raju replied0 replied. "Someone pulled me out of there. Who?"

"I don't know either," Henry said. "I just woke up."

"I'm sorry, Henry," Raju said weakly, tears welling up. "I failed Alexa. I messed up—went in alone. I'm a failure."

"Relax," Henry soothed. "Freshen up first. Uncle Vijay's waiting in the meeting hall—he'll fill you in." Raju nodded, still shaken.

Guilt gnawed at him—he'd broken his promise to save Alexa. Yet Henry seemed oddly calm. Raju's mind lingered on the mysterious savior from the museum.

Fifteen minutes later, they entered the circular meeting hall. Vijay sat in his armchair, clad in a vintage black blazer and slim trousers.

"Sit," Vijay said warmly, gesturing to Raju. He nudged Henry. "Get him some water."

"I think I know what you're about to say," Raju said gravely.

Henry returned with a glass, setting it on the table. Vijay snapped his fingers. "Look at me, Raju."

Raju met his gaze.

"India's your homeland," Vijay began slowly, "but…"

"But what?" Raju murmured.

"Your home is London," Vijay said briskly. Henry and Raju blinked, stunned. "You're Anglo-Indian."

"How do you know that?" Raju asked, astonished.

"You're my son-in-law," Vijay revealed. "Your mother, Diana, is my sister, and your father, Ramnath, was my colleague."

Vijay recounted how Raju had been separated from his parents in India. The revelation answered questions that had haunted Raju since his army days, giving his life new purpose.

"So, Raju's my cousin?" Henry grinned.

"Exactly," Vijay chuckled. "And Raju—Yogi's your cousin too."

"How?" Raju gaped.

"Yogi's mother, Lakshmi, is your father's younger sister," Vijay explained eagerly.

"Raju, remember what you said yesterday?" Henry interjected. "Why you risked it all for Alexa? I felt a connection then—now it's clear!"

"Where are my parents?" Raju asked.

"In Egypt," Vijay replied. "I lost touch after a plane crash twenty years ago. Four years back, I tracked them down. I confirmed you were my nephew after checking your history."

Raju's joy surged, tempered by curiosity.

"You've got a younger brother too," Vijay added, his tone shifting to concern. "You're not alone."

"Who?" Raju pressed.

"Pharaoh," Vijay said. "He saved you last night at the museum. He's a sharp police officer—I tipped him off yesterday."

"Why 'Pharaoh'?" Raju wondered.

"My father's Egyptian," Vijay explained. "He chose that strong name. Yours carries similar weight."

"Where is he?" Raju asked, breathless.

"Wait," Vijay said, glancing at the doorway. "Pharaoh! Your brother's dying to meet you!"

The room hushed. Raju's eyes brimmed with joy—he'd longed for family, and now that wait was over. Pharaoh strode in like a sleek predator, dressed in a sharp black suit, approaching with quiet confidence. Raju felt a jolt seeing him again.

"You—did you try to kill me and Henry three days ago?" Raju demanded.

"No, brother, I saved you," Pharaoh replied with a wry smile.

"What?" Raju stammered.

"Yogi ordered me to kill you," Pharaoh said. "But I already knew who you were. I took out four of his men instead."

"Thanks, bro," Raju said, relieved.

"I saved you last night too," Pharaoh added.

"Let's go, Pharaoh," Raju urged. "We need to save Alexa."

"Relax, brother," Pharaoh said coolly. "She's fine."

"How do you know?" Raju pressed.

"She's in Egypt," Pharaoh answered.

"Egypt?" Henry frowned.

"Yeah," Pharaoh confirmed.

"We heard Yogi kidnapped her," Raju said, skeptical. "What's the point?"

"It was a ruse to lure you," Pharaoh explained. "Uncle Vijay and I sent Alexa to Egypt for research. Yogi's crew was tailing her, but I got her out in time."

"Why all this?" Raju asked, amazed.

"We're secretly studying hidden pyramid chambers with a team of young archaeologists," Vijay said with authority. "Alexa's been sending us data on the crystal chamber daily."

"Crystal chamber?" Henry echoed, intrigued. "Can she really find it?"

"She will," Pharaoh said confidently. "If she does, we'll unlock the capstone's secrets—Khufu's power."

"Alright," Vijay said, sipping his water and setting the glass down. "She'll be back soon."

"Brother," Pharaoh said, his tone brightening, "I've got news."

"Yeah?" Raju nodded.

"Your family—where are they?"

"I've missed them for fourteen years," Raju said flatly. "I heard my wife, Sunehri, and son, Vivek, are here in the city."

"That's what I wanted to tell you!" Pharaoh exclaimed. "Uncle Vijay clued me in on your past. She's an archaeologist now!"

"What?" Raju breathed.

"Yep," Pharaoh said, locking eyes with him. "I've got their address here, but she's in Egypt now. You'll see her soon."

"I want to go to Egypt," Raju said eagerly. "Can you—"

"I'm on it," Pharaoh cut in. "I'll track them down there. Don't worry—you're not alone anymore. We've got your back."

15

The Dream

Raju's sense of isolation began to dissolve the moment Vijay and Pharaoh shared their revelations. Yet a nagging doubt about Alexa's disappearance lingered in his mind.

"Why put Alexa in danger?" he asked Vijay, his tone sharp. "Couldn't you use someone else? I need the real reason."

"I get it," Vijay replied calmly. "She's our expert on the pyramids—the only trustworthy archaeologist we have. If she finds the right spot, our mission wraps up in four days." He clapped his thigh enthusiastically with his left hand.

Raju frowned, unconvinced. "Researching in secret without Yogi interfering seems impossible. He could still hurt her." His thoughts churned with worry for her safety, though he held back from pressing Vijay further.

"What's on your mind, bro?" Pharaoh asked, squinting at Raju's brown eyes. "Yogi couldn't crack that hidden chamber because of you. Now he's desperate to reclaim his pride."

"Exactly," Raju said, a faint grin breaking through.

"Don't worry about Alexa," Vijay cut in briskly. "She's working officially with the Department of Antiquities."

"Mr. Vijay," Raju said, his voice rising, "we all thought the capstone was crystal, but last night I touched it—it's something else. Where's the original? Who took it?"

"No one knows," Pharaoh interjected. "The museum's keeping it hush-hush. I'd bet they swapped it for a fake."

"It's all part of Paramaatma's design," Raju mused. "We need to understand why."

The conversation ended, and they moved to breakfast. Raju, still shaken from the previous night, felt a feverish ache. He retreated to the upstairs verandah, settling onto a bulrush carpet to meditate. Rubbing his palms together, he cupped them over his eyes, then slowly unveiled them, feeling refreshed.

"How are you now?" Henry asked, stepping onto the verandah.

"Good," Raju replied, alert. "The cosmic energy's revived me."

"Is the capstone really that powerful?" Henry pressed.

"It is," Raju said. "Its energy ties into quantum physics—electromagnetic and intra-atomic forces at play."

"Why do people obsess over it?" Henry wondered.

"Those chasing unchecked desires—siddhas—over divine truth lose control in tough times," Raju explained carefully. "Understand?"

"Yeah," Henry nodded. "How does a yogi gain siddhas from God? Is that the right path?"

"No," Raju said. "Those cosmic powers can derail a yogi's journey. Think of God as a Kalpataru—a wish-granting tree from Indian lore. A yogi walks the path, but trouble starts when the tree drops its flowers—siddhas."

"What do you mean?" Henry asked.

"The flowers tempt you," Raju continued. "If you ignore them and reach the tree—God—you find true enlightenment. Pick them up along the way, and you'll miss the real goal."

"Wow," Henry marveled. "That's profound. Thanks, Raju."

"It's my duty to share wisdom for humanity's sake," Raju said, standing.

"How do I meditate to feel God?" Henry asked, echoing a question Raju once posed to his mentor Ishwar. "Where is He?"

"He's beyond words or thought," Raju replied eagerly. "Self-evident—Existence, Knowledge, Bliss: Sath-chith-aanandam. Start by serving society and watching your breath. He's everywhere—in nature, in you, at the core of all beings, their beginning, middle, and end."

"How's God nature?" Henry asked, puzzled.

"He is," Raju said firmly. "His essence spans eight forms: earth, water, fire, air, sky, mind, intellect, ego. That's nature."

Raju's clear answers dispelled Henry's doubts, deepening his respect for Raju's spiritual depth. Still, Raju remained uneasy about Alexa, restless all day.

Night fell quietly, unchanged from before. At 1:00 a.m., while everyone else slept, Raju climbed into bed, switched off the lamp, and pulled a thick blanket over himself. He tossed restlessly before slipping into a deep sleep.

The pyramids gleamed faintly under a massive, diamond-bright full moon. Bats and hawks screeched overhead, their cries piercing the cooling desert air. Misty clouds veiled the glowing Thoth, and dark shadows loomed behind the pyramids and Sun Temple pillars. The golden sand dunes curved like an angel's form, reclining on a bed of gems.

Footsteps echoed suddenly. A young woman— Alexa—raced toward the pyramids through the Sun Temple pillars, her black jeans and white crop-top clinging to her as her reddish-brown hair whipped in the silvery light. She stumbled to Khufu's entrance, sinking to her knees, breathless and drenched in sweat despite the chill. Glancing back, she sensed pursuit.

Clutching a torch in one hand and a revolver in the other, she flicked on the light and loaded five bullets. A distant click made her whip around—nothing.

Shivering, sweat still beading, she muttered, "What's happening? Was Uncle Vijay crazy sending me here, knowing Yogi's after me? This place is insane!"

A thud—a stone dropping—jarred her. "Who's there?" she shouted, aiming her torch.

A shadow brushed her back, hot to the touch. She spun, seeing only its outline morph into a man. He tapped her shoulder, seized her wrist, and forced the gun from her grip. Before she could react, he lunged.

"Aaah!" she screamed. "Raju, save me!"

Raju jolted awake, heart pounding, disoriented. Grabbing his watch by the bed lamp, he saw it was 7:00 a.m.

"Raju!" Henry called, entering with a cheerful "Good morning." He paused, studying Raju's tense face. "Why so rattled?"

"A bad vision," Raju said after a shaky pause. "Alexa's in trouble—hurt by some strange force."

"Just a nightmare," Henry reassured him. "Ignore it. She called me a minute ago."

"What? She's okay?" Raju asked, urgent.

"Yeah," Henry nodded. "Uncle Vijay's sending Pharaoh to Egypt."

16

Smuggling from Egypt

Raju remained unconvinced by Henry's assurances about Alexa. He wanted to discuss his concerns with Pharaoh, though he wavered on whether his astral vision was real. Deep down, he sensed impending danger.

After breakfast, Raju and Henry settled onto a futon in the living room, their eyes glued to the LED TV mounted on the wall as news headlines flashed across the screen.

HEADLINES:

"POLICE PROBE DISAPPEARANCE OF FORMER SECURITY CHIEF OF BRITISH MUSEUM"

"SUPREME COURT BANS OPENING OF 6TH VAULT AT SRI PADMANABHASWAMY TEMPLE IN KERALA"

"INDIAN OCEANOGRAPHERS UNCOVER MYSTERIOUS ANCIENT RUINS ON OCEAN FLOOR IN THE INDIAN OCEAN"

"Fascinating," Raju murmured, spellbound, turning up the volume. "Could be tied to Vishnusamhitha."

"Huh?" Henry asked, wide-eyed.

"A lost kingdom ruled by a stunning queen," Raju explained softly, recounting the tale of Kesika that James had once shared. "If I'm right, a massive crystalline statue might still stand there."

"No way," Henry said, stunned after listening. "I thought it was just a myth. Alexa tried convincing me it was real—I argued with her so many times."

"Now do you see why Yogi's after the capstone?" Raju asked, brow furrowing. "That's what's eating at me."

"Raju, check that out!" Henry pointed to a medium-sized portrait in the corner behind Raju—a striking British woman and a handsome Indian man. "Your mom and dad."

A wide, joyful smile lit up Raju's face as he locked eyes on the old photo. He leapt from the futon, tears of happiness welling as he approached it.

Emma slipped into the room just then, grinning warmly. "Hey."

"Hi, Emma," Henry replied.

"What's Raju staring at so intently?" she asked, nodding toward him.

"His parents," Henry said sincerely. "I'll fill you in later."

"Oh, Pharaoh already told me about them. I'm thrilled to see their picture!" Emma said, her gaze settling on Raju. "Uncle Raju, Mr. Vijay's calling you downstairs."

"Alright, Henry, I'll be back in an hour," Raju said. "Sounds like he's got a lot to say." He left, shutting the door with a soft thud.

"Why doesn't Mr. Vijay ever mock Yogi?" Emma asked Henry, a hint of critique in her tone.

"No clue," Henry shrugged.

"I can imagine how Raju's felt, separated from his parents so long," Emma said gently. "He's incredible."

"He had a nightmare last night," Henry said, voice tight, before recounting Raju's story.

Meanwhile, Raju entered the meeting hall where Vijay was deep in discussion with Pharaoh and three other men.

"Good morning, Raju," Vijay said warmly. "Great to see you."

"Morning, Mr. Vijay."

"This is Iqbal," Vijay said, gesturing to a tall, sallow-skinned man with a sharp nose, dressed in a white shirt and black jeans. "My new assistant. He and Pharaoh are heading to Egypt to disrupt Yogi's operations."

"Pleasure to meet you, Mr. Raju," Iqbal said, offering a firm handshake.

"Sit," Vijay said with a cheerful smirk.

They all took their seats. "Raju," Vijay began.

"Yes?"

"Henry mentioned you're fretting over Alexa," Vijay said. "You can ease up on that."

"Alright," Raju replied, though his tone lacked conviction.

"Pharaoh and Iqbal are off to Egypt," Vijay announced firmly.

"To the pyramids again?" Raju asked.

"No, the airports," Vijay clarified.

"But smuggling slips past police and cameras so easily," Pharaoh said bluntly.

"How do they hide it with such tight security?" Raju asked, curiosity piqued.

"Simple," Pharaoh said with a grin.

"Yet tough to dodge detection," Vijay added softly.

"They coat stolen stone artifacts with gold paint," Pharaoh explained. "It makes them look freshly made— conceals its ancient origin, no one spots the difference."

"Egypt's got tons of stone-carving businesses," Vijay said. "They reshape the relics into Pharaonic faces or other figures, passing them off as new."

"Then they use hydrogen peroxide and ammonia to strip the paint," Pharaoh continued. "Once clear of surveillance, the artifacts regain their original look. That's what we're targeting."

"Yogi's reach goes beyond Egypt," Raju said thoughtfully. "He's hit historical sites worldwide including ancient temples in India. That failed attack on Alexa in Delhi proves he's not after archaeological fame—just control."

"You're right, bro," Pharaoh agreed. "He started with the Valley of the Kings in Luxor, then spread out."

"He's chasing supernatural power," Vijay argued.

"No," Raju countered, meeting Vijay's gaze. "He's courting disaster. We need to crush his confidence."

17

I found that place

"Is Yogi delusional or what? Why's he so sure the crystal chamber exists?" Iqbal asked with a smirk. "Is it even real?"

Henry slipped into the room, curious to catch more of Vijay's conversation with Raju. "Who knows?" Vijay replied.

"I do," came a soft, sweet voice from the doorway. All eyes turned to the entrance.

"Alexa! You're back!" Henry shouted, rushing toward her with uncontainable excitement. She stood there, beaming, and he wrapped her in a tight, joyful hug. "How are you, sis?"

"Let her breathe, Henry," Pharaoh said, chuckling as he watched them.

"I'm great, bro," Alexa replied, her grin wide. Henry released her. "Raju's been a wreck over a nightmare about you last night," he added.

"Hey, ease up, Henry," Vijay interjected warmly. "She's exhausted from the trip—let her rest."

Winter swept into London with a vengeance, chilling its 13 million residents. It was Christmas Eve, December

24th—Alexa's 27th birthday. The villa buzzed with excitement as everyone threw themselves into a lavish celebration.

"Happy birthday, Alexa!" Henry exclaimed, brimming with cheer in his snuff-colored suit. "Come on, cut the cake!"

"Alright," she said, eyeing the tiered cake on the round table by the Christmas tree. Dressed in a sleek black party gown, she glowed.

The terrace sparkled under falling snow, the festivities framed by an eighteen-foot Christmas tree adorned with dazzling decorations. The floor glistened, slick with flurries.

"Many happy returns, my dear," Pharaoh said, shaking her hand before pulling her into a warm hug.

Raju's phone buzzed mid-celebration. He answered. "Hello?"

"Merry Christmas, Raju," a smooth voice greeted. "How are you?"

"Yogi?" Raju said, stunned.

"That's me," Yogi replied.

"Same to you," Raju said, his tone guarded. "What do you want now?"

"Just calling to wish my cousin well," Yogi said lightly.

"Did you always know who I was?" Raju pressed, eager.

"Of course," Yogi said slowly. "Is Alexa safe?"

"Yes," Raju snapped. "Where's my wife?"

"No time for nonsense," Yogi teased, then hung up.

"You bastard," Raju growled, shoving his phone back into his pocket.

"Jingle bell, jingle bell," Alexa began to hum.

"Sing something fresh, Alexa," Henry teased. "That old tune won't trend."

"Shut it, you goof," she shot back playfully.

"Let's get this party going!" Henry declared. Emma joined in, radiant in a gold festive dress.

"Oh, God," Vijay muttered, bored.

"What?" Henry asked.

"Same old routine," Vijay said. "Let's switch it up." The background music shifted.

"Come on, Raju—sing and dance with me and Pharaoh," Alexa urged.

"Gladly," Raju said, his mood lifting. He started to sing:

> *I have to wait for a minute....*
> *you are now making a big mistake....*

I have to say...
You have a way...
do you obey?

Time to end the conflict that you begun...
You have to win the day while you risen...

I have to wait for a minute...

This happened years ago...
You have to go....
When the saga continues...
it's a breaking news...

It's not a right thing....
that you fascinating....

You can do anything...

if you are willing...

I have to wait for a minute....

"Wow, you've got pipes!" Vijay praised. "Keep it up!"

The group erupted in applause, then danced together—Raju, Emma, Henry, and the rest—moving with infectious energy.

"Alexa's happier than ever," Vijay whispered to himself. "Hey, Alexa!"

"Yeah?"

"What do you think of Henry and Emma?" he asked, nodding toward them.

"He found a match early," she said. "They're perfect together."

"And your research?" Raju asked, his face alight with anticipation. "Did you find it?"

"Not here," Pharaoh cut in.

"Right, not the place for big reveals," Alexa agreed, heading downstairs. "To the meeting hall."

"What about Henry?" Raju asked.

"Leave him with Emma," Pharaoh said. "Iqbal, you're with us."

Five of them—Raju, Pharaoh, Iqbal, Vijay, and Alexa—crossed a corridor lit by tiny decorative bulbs and entered the circular conference room. Raju, Pharaoh, and Iqbal settled on a black semicircular daybed, while Vijay and Alexa took armchairs nearby.

"What did you uncover?" Iqbal asked, his gaze steady on Alexa.

"Truth," she said simply.

"What?" Henry and Emma said in unison, stepping into the room.

"The capstone's powers and curses—they're real," Alexa said, her voice heavy with meaning.

"How do you know?" Emma asked gently. "Did you go there?"

"Yes," Alexa began, painting the scene. "It was strange. Ten days ago, on a full moon, I was decoding hieroglyphs on the Sun Temple's walls and pillars in biting cold. A faint scream sent me scrambling into the Great Pyramid. Something touched my back—I passed out from the shock. When I came to, I was an ethereal form, a blazing outline, with a silver cord stretching from my navel to my body, endlessly elastic. I realized it was my astral self."

"English?" Emma said, brushing hair from her face. "What did he say?"

"I was dazed," Alexa continued. "An old man in white robes, radiating light like some heavenly guide, appeared. He spoke ancient Egyptian, but it hit my mind in English—adaptable to any language. He said 'Pharaoh' first, then beckoned me to follow."

"Where'd he take you?" Raju asked.

"Lots of places," she said calmly. "The hidden chamber where the capstone belongs, even back to when it was forged. I asked who he was—he wouldn't say, just gave me three hours with him. Then a kingdom unfolded before me: a princess wed to a grand king, their realm swallowed by the sea, cursed by a cunning wizard, Kesika."

"That's what James told me!" Raju said, awestruck.

"Really?" Alexa nodded, elaborating. "He said the wizard's power lingers in the capstone, waiting to resurface. Vivékadeva's alive, trapped in a crystalline statue. I saw the Great Pyramid being built—levitation lifted those huge stones, no ramps needed, up to its glowing white peak. He also told me about the existence of the Hall Of Records underneath the Sphinx! He led me through the slippery burial chamber, past the King's chamber, to a wide corridor with rosy walls lit by the glow of my astral body. We reached a massive door. 'This is it,' he said. 'Go through without looking back— that's how you'll find the truth.'"

"I was nervous," she admitted, "but I stepped through into the hidden chamber. Diamond-encrusted walls sparkled blindingly. I wondered where the capstone fit, so I turned to ask him. Instantly, an unseen force yanked me back to my body faster than light. When I came to, I checked my watch—midday, December 23rd. Nine days had vanished!"

"Time travel?" Emma speculated.

"Not quite," Alexa said. "An astral journey."

"You slept nine days in the pyramid?" Henry asked, incredulous.

"Felt like three hours," she replied.

"How?" Henry pressed, enthralled.

"Only the Great Pyramid bends time like that," Vijay explained. "Mass and time balance there—time slows compared to elsewhere. No paradoxes. Alexa slipped into the future."

"Genius," Henry muttered.

"She found the easiest way in," Raju said, impressed.

Emma's phone rang then. "Hello?" she answered softly. Her face darkened within seconds. "NOOOOO!!!" she cried out in anguish.

18

My Grandfather's Diary

Emma hurled her phone to the floor, the device shattering into fragments as she collapsed, sobbing uncontrollably, her hands pressed to her face.

"Emma, what's wrong?" Henry rushed to her side, his voice thick with concern.

"Tom," she choked out between tears. "He's dead!"

"What?" Vijay's voice boomed, incredulous.

"Yogi killed him," Emma spat, her grief twisting into fury. "Because he knew who Tom was. He tried to kill me too!"

"When did this happen?" Raju asked, his tone steady but urgent.

"I don't know," Emma stammered, her nerves fraying. "Please, Uncle Raju—kill him!"

"Don't cry, Emma," Alexa soothed, resting a hand on her shoulder.

"He took everything," Emma wailed. "He caused Mom's death at the World Trade Center, Dad vanished, and now he's murdered my brother!"

"We'll stop him," Alexa said calmly. "The capstone will be his end."

"She's right," Vijay agreed, taking Emma's trembling hand in his weathered grip to offer comfort.

The next morning, Vijay and Pharaoh strode down the corridor toward Raju's bedroom. Pharaoh wore an olive-hooded T-shirt and black jeans, while Vijay was sharp in a black suit. Sunlight streamed across the floor in golden bands.

"Rise and shine, bro," Pharaoh called, rapping lightly on the door.

"Over here!" Raju replied, stepping in from the lawn. "Looking for me?"

"We've got something big to share," Vijay said with a grin. "Come along."

"Morning, everyone," Alexa greeted, approaching from a distance in a cotton tee and shorts. "What's special today?"

"Yogi's invited us to his place for a New Year's party," Pharaoh said coolly.

"What's our move?" Alexa asked, tension creeping into her voice.

"We'll see," Vijay replied.

"He killed Emma's brother," Alexa pointed out. "We can't trust him."

"He didn't," Vijay muttered, fixing her with a hard stare.

"What did you say?" Raju asked, stunned.

"I don't think he did it—not if he's after that power," Vijay explained. "I'll tell you why in a moment. Follow me."

They entered Vijay's bedroom, a shadowy sanctum with dark walls adorned with family portraits tracing his lineage. Bronze statues from cultures worldwide gleamed in the corners, including a striking Nataraja— Shiva as the cosmic dancer.

Vijay gestured to a portrait of a bearded elderly man. "My grandfather, Ahmed," he said, nodding to Pharaoh. "From my mother's side." He lifted the frame from the wall, revealing a small hidden door. "In you go."

Pharaoh ducked into the ten-foot tunnel and emerged with a weathered, mildew-streaked wooden box. "Set it here," Vijay instructed, tapping a desk at the room's center. Pharaoh placed it down, brushing away cobwebs with a velvet cloth. Vijay produced a robotic key, its mechanism whirring as it adjusted to the lock's intricate pattern.

"Got it!" Alexa exclaimed as the box clicked open. "Let's see."

Pharaoh eased the lid up. "There it is," Vijay murmured, his excitement palpable as he lifted a bundle of parchment from within.

"What's that?" Alexa asked.

"Grandfather's diary," Vijay replied.

"Anything crucial in there?" she pressed.

"Absolutely," Vijay said, flipping it open to read aloud:

March 21, 1923—a day etched in my soul. I embarked on an ethereal voyage into a realm of unveiled mysteries. For nearly a month, I roamed a subconscious tapestry of past and present.

A man guided me to an immortal plane. "The tale of Kesika and his capstone dates to 3,102 B.C., known to all." The key lies in who wields it beneath the cosmic energy's electromagnetic veil. That soul must master their deepest desires, wielding self-restraint and spiritual clarity.

Fail these virtues, and they'll face eternal torment, enslaved by the wizard Kesika, bound to his will within their own flesh. When the dream turns real, past becomes present—marked by the full moon, revealed on the new moon."

"What's it mean?" Pharaoh asked.

"It's a roadmap to the exact day this unfolds," Vijay said. "Alexa's full-moon experience tipped us off."

"No," Raju cut in sharply. "She confirmed what I already sensed. Today's the new moon—now it's clear. The full moon's January 8th."

"Fourteen days," Alexa calculated. "So, Uncle Vijay, about Yogi killing Tom—"

Vijay's phone rang, cutting her off. He answered. "Hello?"

"Uncle Vijay! How are you?" a smooth voice chimed.

"Yogi—what a surprise," Vijay replied dryly. "What do you want?"

"To clear something up about Tom," Yogi said. "I didn't kill him."

"Is that true?" Vijay asked, skeptical.

"Yes," Yogi insisted. "Pharaoh did."

"What the hell are you saying?" Vijay snapped.

"Don't fume—it's a fact," Yogi said calmly. "The day Alexa was taken, he died in a car explosion with four of my men. Pharaoh's work."

"Your men tried to kill Raju and Henry," Vijay shot back.

"Fair point—a cop's duty to shield the innocent," Yogi said slyly. "No mistake there. Tell Pharaoh to drop the James Thomson case. I've got the last witness."

"Who?" Vijay barked, but the line went dead.

"Uncle Vijay!" Henry burst in, breathless. "Emma's gone—she left this!" He thrust a note into Vijay's hand.

Vijay scanned it, his face falling. "A suicide note. Damn it."

"What now?" Alexa asked, her voice trembling.

"We save her," Pharaoh said, resolute.

19

A vivacious chase

"Henry," Raju said, his voice low and deliberate.

"Yeah?" Henry replied, turning to him.

"Last night, Emma seemed off—moody, weighed down by something," Raju began.

"It's because of Tom's death," Vijay interjected, cutting him off.

"No, Mr. Vijay," Raju countered, shaking his head. "I saw her just an hour ago, before you came to my room. She was happy—almost relieved."

"What?" Alexa's brow furrowed in confusion.

"I spoke to her about her father's disappearance," Raju explained, his tone softening. "It happened that night three months ago at the British Museum, when I fought off Yogi's men. She's the last piece of evidence to nail him. This isn't suicide—it's a kidnapping."

"How can you be so sure?" Vijay asked, his eyes narrowing.

"She wanted Yogi dead," Pharaoh said, his voice steady.

"Where is she?" Henry shouted, panic rising.

"Easy, Henry," Pharaoh said, giving him a light slap on the shoulder. "I've handled cases like this before. We're not too late—let's move."

"Wait!" Alexa called, darting upstairs. "I need to change."

"It's freezing out there," Pharaoh noted. "Dress like a spy."

"Your wish is my command," she shot back with a quick grin.

Leaving Vijay behind, they descended to the car shed. Pharaoh slid into the driver's seat, Alexa beside him, while Raju and Henry settled in the back. They scoured nearby lanes, eventually reaching the site of the car explosion near The Tower Bridge. Raju recounted to Alexa and Pharaoh how Henry had saved his life that day, pulling him from the car just in time.

As their sedan neared the bridge, Alexa's gaze drifted to its towering silhouette. Pharaoh's phone buzzed, breaking the silence.

"Hello?" he answered, tension edging his voice.

"It's Clint. Where are you, Mr. Pharaoh?" came the reply.

"Approaching The Tower Bridge," Pharaoh said.

"We've got trouble," Clint said urgently. "A rogue vehicle's tearing through from Westminster to London, endangering lives right where you are. Stop it."

"Got it, sir," Pharaoh said, ending the call.

"Look out!" Alexa and Henry cried in unison.

A black-and-white Volvo bus barreled into their path, slamming their car with a jarring thud. The sedan teetered on the bridge's edge, inches from the parapet. Raju grabbed Henry's collar and yanked him out, both plunging into the river below. Pharaoh and Alexa scrambled to the back seat, leaping into the air as the impact flung them free. They latched onto the bus's front, shattering its mirrors, while their car crumpled beneath the bus's massive tires.

"Hold on tight, Alexa!" Pharaoh shouted. "We need to climb up!"

"On it," she gritted out.

"Who's the idiot driving this thing?" Pharaoh growled. "We've got to stop him—now."

They smashed through the bus's windows, landing inside amidst a group of armed figures. Pharaoh drew his revolver, slamming the butt into a masked man's head. Alexa lunged at the driver, kicking him out the door and seizing the wheel. Pharaoh tackled another thug, knocking him flat.

A muffled "Hmmm" rose from a figure tied in a gunny sack nearby. "Ahhh," it groaned as Pharaoh approached.

Four men swarmed Alexa, wrenching her from the driver's seat. The bus veered wildly, but she fought back with fierce determination. Pharaoh tore open the sack, revealing Emma—bound in metal wires, her mouth taped shut, writhing in pain.

"Emma!" he exclaimed, swiftly freeing her after dispatching her captors. Alexa broke free too, but her eyes widened as the bus careened toward the bridge's edge.

Pharaoh's task doubled: save Emma and Alexa. Hoisting Emma onto his back, he grabbed Alexa's waist and hauled her toward the exit. They leapt just as the bus smashed into the parapet, obliterating the concrete barrier. The vehicle spun backward, plummeting into the Thames with a thunderous explosion, flames and debris scattering across the water.

They hit the river hard, Pharaoh's grip unwavering even in chaos. Swimming clear of the wreckage, they watched the bus's fragments sink behind them.

"Thank God," Alexa gasped, relief flooding her voice. "We're alive."

"You okay, Emma?" Pharaoh asked, treading water.

"Yeah," she replied, her voice shaky from the cold. "Thank you, Pharaoh—you've filled the void Tom left." She clung to him in a grateful embrace.

"Look!" Alexa pointed. A river guard's speedboat sliced through the water, Henry and Raju aboard.

"There you are!" Henry called as the boat pulled alongside. "Get in!"

"Good to see you, Emma," Raju said warmly, clapping her shoulder. "Well done, you two," he added, nodding to Alexa and Pharaoh.

"What happened, sir?" the river guard asked.

"My brother Pharaoh and his fiancée Alexa just saved a sharp young woman," Raju said with a cool smile. Pharaoh and Alexa exchanged a glance, grinning.

"Emma's no innocent—she's clever as hell," Henry chimed in, his enthusiasm infectious.

20

Back To Egypt

"We're all going to Egypt," Vijay declared with conviction after Raju recounted the latest events. They sat on wooden benches in the villa's front yard, the turf soft beneath their feet. Iqbal ran a hand through his hair, smoothing it absently.

"Egypt?" Henry echoed, brows lifting.

"Yes, Henry—Egypt," Vijay confirmed. "We need to thwart Yogi's final move. He's not the mastermind he seems—too reliant on someone else's guidance."

Pharaoh nodded. "We've got to figure out who's pulling his strings."

"Who might that be?" Emma asked, her voice tentative.

"Vikram, perhaps?" Vijay ventured. "Yogi couldn't pull this off without an elder's help—maybe his grandfather, Amarnath."

"No way," Pharaoh countered. "Vikram's not the type to drag his son into pseudoscience. He's living out his days as an ascetic somewhere in India."

"Fine," Vijay conceded. "It's less about who's helping him and more about stopping him. Pack up—we're catching the evening flight."

"Uncle Vijay, I'll join you in Egypt later," Pharaoh said.

"Me too," Iqbal mumbled.

"Something urgent?" Vijay asked.

"Yeah," Pharaoh replied. "I'm off to Sri Lanka with my team to transfer ancient ruins to the Cairo Museum."

"Take care, then," Vijay said, patting his knee. Pharaoh and Iqbal left together. "Let's get ready, everyone," Vijay added, dialing his assistant to secure flight tickets.

The afternoon dragged on, heavy with a drowsy stillness. As the sun dipped into the Thames, flocks of birds returned to their riverbank nests. Vijay, Raju, Alexa, Henry, and Emma waited at the airport. The plane touched down at last, and they boarded one by one, settling into their seats. Hours later, it landed at Cairo International Airport in the predawn chill.

"Freezing!" Emma shivered.

"Wait till midday—it'll scorch," Alexa said, her tone flat as she glanced at a sign overhead: Welcome to Al-Qāhirah.

One of Vijay's assistants arrived in a car, whisking them to the official residence of the Antiquities Department.

Sunrise painted Cairo gold as Ra rose over the Nile, banishing the night's bite with warmth. Vijay's phone buzzed. He answered.

"Buenos días, sir," a shaky voice said in Spanish. "Yo tener un importante aspecto a decir vosotros."

"¿Lo ser qué?" Vijay replied, irritation creeping in.

"Él ser en Cairo."

"Yo hacer no escuchar alguna cosa lo tal vez cualquier menos le Martin," Vijay snapped, cutting the call.

"Who was that, Uncle Vijay?" Henry asked, stepping into the room. "You look rattled."

"Nothing—just a colleague," Vijay lied, forcing a smile. "I've got a surprise for you, Henry."

Henry froze, eyeing Vijay's enigmatic expression without a word.

"Your dad's coming today," Vijay revealed.

"Why didn't he tell me?" Henry muttered, though Vijay caught it.

"I called him yesterday—invited him to spend the winter break here," Vijay explained.

"Brilliant," Henry said, softening. "He's always too busy when I ask. Thanks for convincing him, Uncle Vijay."

"I'm his big brother," Vijay teased. "He has to listen to me." The jest carried a subtle lesson about respect, one Henry mulled over, wondering why Vijay chose now to impart it—and what entanglement he might be missing.

"Breakfast yet?" Vijay asked.

"Nope," Henry replied.

"Then let's go—Alexa's probably waiting downstairs."

They entered the dining room, where Raju, Alexa, and Emma already sat.

"Morning, Raju!" Vijay greeted. Raju nodded with a warm smile. "I'm feeling good today—something's in the air."

"Something great's coming," Alexa said, almost to herself. "And—"

"Dad's on his way," Henry cut in.

"I knew before you did," Alexa shot back. "He'll be here soon."

"I sent my assistant to the airport an hour ago," Vijay said.

Honk! Honk!

"That's them!" Alexa exclaimed, bounding up. "Raju, come meet him!"

Henry flung open the door and stepped onto the porch as the car rolled to a stop. "Hi, Dad!"

"Hey, Henry!" John emerged—blue-eyed, brown-haired, a geologist and newspaper editor from Los Angeles, exuding the same gravitas as Vijay. "How's my boy?"

"Good, Dad," Henry said.

"I missed you so much," Alexa said, rushing forward to hug him tightly.

"Me too, sweetheart," John replied, squeezing her back.

"Dad, this is Raju," Alexa said, gesturing.

"I've heard about you from Alexa's adventure tales," John said, extending a hand. "Nice to meet you, Raju. I'm John."

"Likewise," Raju replied, shaking it firmly.

"Come in, John," Vijay called from the doorway. "We've got something big to discuss."

"What's up?" John asked.

"Freshen up first—then I'll fill you in," Vijay said.

Raju and Alexa exchanged puzzled glances, unsettled by Vijay's sudden shift in demeanor. Henry, oblivious, basked in his father's arrival, introducing Emma as his friend and regaling John with their antics—like the time she'd caught him rifling through her wallet.

"He's forgotten us," Alexa grumbled, watching them. "Totally smitten with her."

"It's just friendship," Raju said gently. "He's hurting but won't open up to us—too young to lean on elders. Emma's his lifeline."

"True," Alexa agreed. "She's his only real friend."

John laughed as Henry recounted getting walloped for the wallet stunt. "Henry used to think he was London's slickest kid—overconfidence galore. She's tamed that."

"By who?" Henry asked, bristling slightly, then grinned as he realized his dad approved of Emma.

"Good pick, son," John whispered. "Look at your sister—she's jealous."

Henry glanced at Alexa, her cheeks flushed. "Chill, Alexa," he teased. "You're just mad you don't have a friend like mine."

"Lame, you dork," she fired back, grinning as she followed him inside.

Breakfast wrapped up with Vijay, John, Henry, Raju, Alexa, and Emma at the table.

"Raju, can you take us to the Egyptian Museum?" Henry asked.

"Sure," Raju said.

"Great idea," Vijay said, though his energy lagged.

"You two coming, Uncle Vijay?" Alexa asked, standing.

"No, dear—we've got work," Vijay replied. "You go ahead."

"Cool—we'll grab lunch out," Alexa said.

"Whatever you like," Vijay agreed.

"Thanks, Uncle Vijay!" she chirped.

"Be safe," John added with a smile.

Raju, Alexa, Henry, and Emma stepped outside. Henry eyed Vijay's car on the porch, but Raju ignored it, striding past.

"Car?" Henry asked briskly.

"No," Raju said firmly. "We'll take a cab."

Henry nodded, recalling Yogi's last attack, and followed Raju to the bustling main road. Raju flagged a cab.

"Aap ko kahaa jaana hai?" the driver asked in Urdu.

"Egyptian Museum," Raju replied. They piled into the cramped cab and set off.

Date palms lined the route as they passed Cairo Tower, the Qahira Fatimid Mosque, and Downtown's smog-choked streets, thick with hydrocarbon haze. At last, they reached Tahrir Square, ringed by administrative buildings, and stopped at the museum's courtyard.

The place teemed with visitors, security tight yet strained. People jostled in line, driven by a feverish urge to glimpse ancient wonders.

Raju's group entered the ground floor, marveling at alabaster vases, papyrus scrolls, and coins from antiquity.

"Upstairs has bigger stuff—1550 to 1069 BC," Alexa said, pointing to a massive sarcophagus. "Let's go."

"You've been here before," Emma noted.

"Yeah," Alexa confirmed.

The first floor dazzled with 3,500 artifacts, millennia old. Henry gaped at King Tut's golden mask. "Pure gold—eleven kilos," Alexa said.

"You should be a curator here," Henry joked.

"The royal mummy room's next—twenty-seven Pharaonic mummies," she said.

"Looks limited," Raju observed. "Only nine on display."

"Two got trashed in last year's revolution," Alexa explained.

Raju studied a caged sarcophagus. "Queen Hatshepsut, 14th century BC," Alexa said. "Famous for her Punt expeditions—the 'Land of Gods.'"

"India?" Raju asked. She nodded.

"Some new artifacts just arrived," Henry said, uncertain. "I overheard Uncle Vijay on the phone this morning."

"Really?" Alexa asked. "What?"

"No idea," Henry admitted.

"We should ask the curator," Emma suggested.

Raju agreed, scanning for staff. "Excuse me," he called to a thin man nearby.

"I'd like to see the curator," Raju said, sharing their details.

"Wait here—I'll get him," the man replied, darting off and returning shortly. "This way, sir."

They followed him to the curator's office. He left them at the glass door, which Raju pushed open.

"Come in," a deep voice beckoned.

Raju stepped inside, the room untidy but fragrant with jasmine. A tall man of seventy stood by the window, back to them. The others filed in.

"What do you want?" the man asked, his tone commanding.

"We're here about the mysterious capstone," Alexa said swiftly.

"Which one?" he pressed.

"Kesika's," Raju replied.

"I'll tell you," the man said, turning slowly. Raju's breath caught—he knew that face from a portrait at Vijay's villa, a younger version beside a British woman. It was Ramnath.

"Dad," Raju whispered, joy swelling in his chest. The room froze, stunned—including Ramnath himself.

21

The sword of Vivékadeva

Overwhelmed with joy, Ramnath's face lit up with a wide smile, his eyes glistening with tears of happiness as he recalled cherished memories. He opened his arms warmly toward Raju, and the two embraced tightly.

In that moment, Raju felt all his worries melt away. He bent down to touch his father's feet in a gesture of respect, and Ramnath placed his hands on Raju's head, blessing him. As Raju stood, Ramnath gripped his shoulders gently and said, "I'm so proud of you, my son!" Gratitude flooded Raju's heart as he silently thanked the divine.

Henry, Alexa, and Emma shared in the happiness of the reunion, with Emma beaming at the sight. They introduced themselves to Ramnath, and Raju recounted the many challenges he had faced. The group gathered around a table, where Alexa briefly updated Ramnath on the situation with the capstone.

"How can we stop its consequences?" she asked, her voice tinged with concern. "It feels beyond our control—like the world is in grave danger!"

"It's not as hopeless as you think," Ramnath replied calmly. "Every problem has a solution."

"What do you mean, Uncle Ramnath?" Henry pressed.

"There's something that determines who is worthy of the capstone's power," Ramnath explained.

"What is it?" Henry asked eagerly.

"The sword of Vivékadeva," Ramnath said softly. "It alone decides. But we still have a chance."

"I've heard a little about this sword six months ago," Raju said, puzzled. "Does it have the power to kill?"

"No, it wasn't created to take lives," Ramnath clarified. "It was a test—a measure of whether someone is truly human. Vivékadeva subjected himself to it as well. Unfortunately, Kesika exploited that opportunity…"

A heavy silence fell over the room, each person absorbed in curiosity about what had happened.

"There's a mystery here, isn't there?" Emma ventured, intrigued.

"Not quite," Ramnath replied. "It's more of an open secret. These trials aren't meant for those ruled by the six inner enemies—lust, anger, selfishness, madness, greed, and envy."

"So Kesika sought out such people," Raju deduced.

"Exactly," Ramnath confirmed. "He can only merge with someone corrupt."

"That's his purpose?" Henry asked.

"Yes," Ramnath said. "It's how he vanishes into a wicked host. That's why he needs them."

"That's chilling," Henry murmured.

"But Vivékadeva was far wiser," Ramnath continued. "He foresaw this long ago. We still have a choice."

"How could he predict that?" Emma asked skeptically.

"Come with me," Ramnath said, cutting her off. He rose swiftly and headed for the door.

They followed him to a vast underground chamber beneath the museum, shrouded in darkness. He stopped before an iron platform, where a massive, shadowy object stood, faintly illuminated and guarded by laser beams.

"What is this?" Alexa whispered, awestruck.

Ramnath flipped on the lights, revealing a towering, rhombus-shaped crystalline rock—13 feet tall—glimmering brilliantly. Inside, a human silhouette shimmered faintly, resembling Vivékadeva's form.

"It's incredible!" Raju gasped, hardly believing his eyes. "Vivékadeva's body—it's still here!"

"It's one of archaeology's greatest finds," Alexa exclaimed.

"We scanned it last night," Ramnath said, gesturing toward the rock. "He's still youthful!"

"What?" Raju said, stunned. "His body hasn't decayed?"

"No," Ramnath replied with conviction. "That's why I say he's an extraordinary being."

"When was this discovered?" Alexa asked. "Where did it come from?"

"For 30 years, Indo-Egyptian archaeologists, alongside expert oceanographers, searched the Indian Ocean," Ramnath explained. "They found it last week near the Sri Lankan plate."

"But there's no evidence of a sunken landmass there," Alexa said, nodding thoughtfully. "How is that possible?"

"You're right—geologically, there's no trace," Ramnath agreed. "Yet it once existed. Ancient Egyptian scripts claim the kingdom of Vishnusamhita was obliterated by Kesika's cataclysm—except for this rock."

"Amazing," Alexa breathed.

"Vivékadeva achieved immortality," Ramnath said. "Nothing can destroy his body. Kesika couldn't kill him outright, so he cursed him, trapping him in this unbreakable crystal to immobilize him."

"Kesika feared him," Raju said firmly. "That's why he hid in the capstone like a trapped spirit."

"Is he still alive?" Henry asked nervously.

"Yes," Ramnath nodded. "But he's bound in that stone forever—unless it's broken."

"Are you planning to break it?" Raju asked, intrigued.

"No," Ramnath said with a smile, patting Raju's shoulder. "Not me, not Vijay, not Yogi. It's you and Pharaoh."

Raju froze, struck by the weight of his father's words. Questions swirled in his mind. Why break the rock? Was it tied to the capstone? He gazed at Ramnath, seeking answers.

"I suggest you and Pharaoh place the capstone in the Great Pyramid," Ramnath said decisively. "Will you do it, son?"

"But, Dad," Raju replied, hesitant yet trusting, "how do you know I'm worthy?"

"You're spiritually awakened," Ramnath said warmly. "My brother Ishwar wrote to me about your growth. Pharaoh, too, is a master of the occult and self-realized."

"What about Kesika's influence?" Raju asked.

"When the power goes to the righteous, Kesika loses his hold," Ramnath assured him. "He'll dissolve into the universe."

Henry and Emma stared at Vivékadeva's silhouette, captivated, while Alexa turned to Ramnath. "Has anyone searched for his sword?"

"Yes," Ramnath replied. "In April 1966, four British archaeologists uncovered it in an abandoned mastaba— later identified as the tomb of Kesika's disciple."

"Where is it now?" she pressed.

"I don't know," Ramnath admitted. "I suspect it was stolen before reaching the British Museum."

"Dad, the museum's security chief, James Thomson, told me the same," Raju added. "Artifacts vanish before they're secured. Yogi wasn't the first."

"Who were the archaeologists?" Emma asked, turning to Ramnath.

He paused, taking a deep breath. "I was one of them."

"What?" Alexa exclaimed, wide-eyed. Raju's excitement surged.

"The others?" Raju urged.

"Diana, my wife," Ramnath said slowly. "Then Amarnath."

"This is confusing!" Alexa burst out. "Yogi's grandfather, a criminal, an archaeologist? Wasn't he sentenced to death for killing police during an escape?"

"Let me clarify," Ramnath said gently. "That's not true. Amarnath was a suspect in the sword's disappearance, but Diana and I were in India then, leaving Raju with Ishwar when he was eight months old."

"Oh," Raju said softly. "And the fourth?"

"Vijay," Ramnath replied, locking eyes with Raju.

The room buzzed with shock. Raju's mind raced, piecing together the puzzle.

"Dad, how did Vijay become a London icon as a jailer?" Raju asked.

"Jailer?" Ramnath chuckled darkly. "A lie. He began as an archaeologist. Amarnath led the team."

"What?" Alexa gasped.

"Vijay was my junior," Ramnath explained. "Diana introduced him—her younger brother—after he finished his Egyptology degree at Oxford."

"So Vijay framed Amarnath to escape blame?" Alexa asked.

"Yes," Ramnath confirmed. "He pinned the theft on him."

"Where was Vikram?" Henry interjected.

"In India with us, for his wedding to my sister Lakshmi," Ramnath said.

"Why didn't Amarnath attend his son's wedding?" Raju asked. "How did Vijay frame him?"

"We trusted Vijay," Ramnath said. "He stayed with Amarnath, who was tasked with guarding the sword. It vanished the next day, before leaving Egypt. Amarnath searched everyone—except Vijay."

"Why not him?" Raju pressed.

"Amarnath saw him as his son's loyal friend and assistant," Ramnath said. "That blind trust was his mistake."

"So Vijay lied to me to hide the truth," Raju realized, troubled.

"He kidnapped me when I got close to it," Emma added. "Pharaoh and Alexa saved me, but I couldn't speak until now."

"I suspected Vijay was targeting us," Raju said. "Now it's clear."

"I was terrified when Pharaoh said you were at Vijay's villa," Ramnath admitted, relieved. "Did anyone know you came to see me?"

"We didn't even know you'd be here," Raju replied. "Vijay only knew we were visiting the museum."

"Where's Pharaoh?" Ramnath asked, suddenly tense.

"He called this morning," Alexa said. "He's back in London from Sri Lanka."

22

An expected commandeer

"Is he coming here today?" Alexa asked, her voice tinged with curiosity.

"I don't know for sure!" came the honest reply from her friend. "But, Uncle Ramnath, why do you look so nervous?"

Ramnath's brow furrowed as he explained, "The Egyptian government has decided to reclaim artifacts from around the globe! And yet, there's no real security here to safeguard those treasures. Everything's under Yogi's control now—it'd be a cakewalk to swipe them here." His tone was resolute. "Even the capstone!"

"No security at all?" Alexa questioned skeptically. "Are you saying Pharaoh's personally escorting the capstone here by plane?"

"Exactly," Ramnath confirmed with conviction. "There's no police presence like there used to be at the archaeological sites. Now it's just strangers—Yogi's men—lurking around the monuments with guns, waiting for an opportunity. Every morning, I brace myself for the latest report: what's been looted today? What's gone missing?"

"What a critical moment!" Alexa exclaimed, her anxiety bubbling over.

"Yogi might snatch up the world's physical treasures," Raju interjected, clenching his massive fist in frustration, "but he'll never touch the spiritual wealth."

"Come on, Raju! Let's head home for lunch," Ramnath said warmly. "Diana will be thrilled to see you all."

"We're ready, Dad!" Raju grinned, his face lighting up.

They filed out of the room and headed toward the main entrance. The blistering sun had driven most visitors away, leaving the area quiet. Ramnath strode to the parking lot, pulled his sedan out, and paused at the gate. "Hey, kids! Hop in!"

Meanwhile, an airliner from Britain soared toward Cairo, laden with ancient artifacts and guarded by fifteen commandos, led by Pharaoh. It was the very flight Ramnath had been anticipating.

"Why are they hassling us over this?" Iqbal grumbled, seated beside Pharaoh. "This old junk's useless!"

"Easy, my friend," Pharaoh replied calmly. "It's their job to protect these treasures. They're aiming to boost tourism with them."

"You're defending them a bit too much, don't you think?" Iqbal shot back.

"Why so gloomy? Optimism's the way to go in times like these," Pharaoh advised. "It'll all work out."

"Sean!" Iqbal barked.

"Yeah?" Sean replied, irritation creeping into his voice.

"Tell the pilot to ease up on the engines."

"What for?" Pharaoh asked, puzzled.

The plane had just crossed the Mediterranean and entered Egyptian airspace, cutting through the western desert.

"Too much air traffic," Iqbal said with a strained smirk.

"We've passed Alexandria, I think," Pharaoh muttered, noticing a flicker of relief on Iqbal's tense face. Then, his gaze shifted—half the commandos were moving toward the cockpit.

Pharaoh leapt to intervene, but it was too late. Gunshots rang out as the traitors executed both pilots and seized control. He whirled back to Iqbal, slamming the butt of his pistol into his head. Iqbal crumpled but stayed conscious. The loyal commandos opened fire on the turncoats, and chaos erupted.

Bullets tore through the cabin—windows shattered, seats ripped apart, and wind howled through the wreckage. Pharaoh drew his handgun, dropped three of the mutineers, and bolted toward the cargo hold.

The remaining guards fought fiercely to protect the artifacts, but Pharaoh returned swiftly, a machine gun in hand and a parachute strapped to his back. He mowed down the attackers without hesitation.

A figure emerged from the cockpit, lobbing a grenade into the fray. Pharaoh shouted a warning, urging his team to jump. One by one, they leapt from the plane in a frantic five-second scramble. Pharaoh went last.

Boom!

The grenade detonated, flipping the aircraft violently as Pharaoh dove out the rear exit. His parachute deployed, but the canopy snagged on the tail wing, yanking him back. The plane spiraled toward the desert, dragging him along. His face whipped in the wind, his hair flailing, and smoke from the burning cockpit choked his lungs.

He clawed at the brake loop, but it tore free. The pilot chute was useless—torn stabilizer, severed lines. The jet plummeted toward the sand.

Pharaoh shut his eyes, focusing on his breath. Then, in an instant, a miracle—he vanished, teleporting away as the plane slammed into a massive sandbank along the Nile, skidding into the river with a thunderous splash.

Moments later, Pharaoh broke the water's surface, gasping for air. He scanned his surroundings, stunned by the ordeal, and realized he wasn't far from the Great Pyramid. Exhausted, he swam against the current, reaching the Giza plateau as the sun dipped low, painting the sky with twilight.

He clawed onto the riverbank, digging his fingers into the wet sand, and hauled himself up, panting heavily. The pyramid loomed in the fading light. He tried to stand but collapsed, his strength drained. His eyes fluttered shut as he surrendered to sleep on the damp shore.

23

The Killjoy of a relative

"Have some tea, son," Diana said, her eyes sparkled with a quiet joy as she pressed a steaming cup of tea into Raju's hands; her voice a soft melody of warmth.

"Thank you, Mom," Raju replied, his gaze lingering on the familiar creases etched into her face—lines that told stories of resilience and love.

"Pharaoh entered our lives seventeen years after you were born," Diana mused, her tone bright with nostalgia. "I missed you terribly, my boy."

Raju's lips curved into a faint smile as he shared the weight of his solitude, a tapestry woven with threads of longing and fleeting divine revelations.

"Aunt Diana," Alexa ventured, her voice cutting through the tender exchange.

"Yes, honey?" Diana turned, her attention shifting like sunlight through a window.

"How has Kesika's soul endured in the capstone for five thousand years?"

Diana's eyes gleamed with the spark of hidden knowledge. "Do you know of the silver cord?"

"A little," Alexa replied, curiosity piqued. "What's its role?"

"It's everything," Diana said, her words deliberate. "Kesika and Vivékadeva were adepts of Kaayakalpa. Kesika, being a wizard of profound discipline, wove his silver cord into the capstone's very atoms, biding his time for the perfect moment."

Ramnath's voice broke the spell, firm yet eager. "Take a look at this." He unfurled a weathered parchment across the table, its edges curling like ancient secrets. The diagram revealed the Cheops pyramid's hidden veins, with the capstone's energy mapped in precise lines—three vectors converging downward to a triangle's peak, eight more radiating outward in a starburst of force. "It's the binding energy of nucleons," he explained, his finger tracing the ink.

Emma leaned in, her mind alight. "So, the cosmic energy destabilizes the nucleons, pushing him free from the capstone. That's nuclear physics at its core."

"Brilliant," Henry murmured, his voice a low rumble of awe.

Ramnath tapped a void above the king's chamber. "This might be it—the crystal chamber could lie here."

"That's not our true concern, Dad," Raju interjected, his tone steady as stone. "We must thwart that wizard— and Yogi—before it's too late."

"Patience, son," Ramnath counseled, his words a balm. "Destiny finds us all."

"What do you mean?" Raju's brow furrowed.

"You understand why we brought Vivékadeva's idol to the Cairo Museum," Ramnath said, his gaze piercing. "Don't you?"

"Perhaps it aligns with Kesika's emergence?"

"Precisely," Ramnath affirmed. "When Kesika rises, the capstone unleashes a tremor. If the idol's near, it could shatter."

"A curse?" Emma's voice trembled with the question.

"No," Ramnath declared, his voice ringing with purpose. "Our plan."

Raju's breath caught. "What?"

"This is our life's pursuit, son," Ramnath said, his words heavy with conviction. "To liberate Vivékadeva is our sole hope."

"Is that feasible, Uncle Ramnath?" Alexa pressed, her eyes searching his.

"I can't predict the outcome," he confessed, pausing. "But—"

"But what?"

"We need the sword."

"You said it was lost!" Alexa's frustration flared. "What use is it then?"

"It can sever Kesika's silver cord," Ramnath replied, unflinching.

"By cutting it?" Raju's skepticism sharpened his tone.

"Yes," Ramnath said. "And only Vivékadeva can wield it as it must be wielded."

"Where is it, then?" Emma interjected, her glance darting to Raju. "Yogi might already have it."

"Perhaps," Raju conceded. "That would explain his confidence."

"If my intuition is right," Alexa said, her voice taut with intensity, "Uncle Vijay has it."

"Then we go to him," Raju decided, rising with resolve. "We must hurry."

Diana and Ramnath exchanged a glance freighted with unease, but Raju's determination was a tide they couldn't stem. He led his team back to the hotel.

***

"Good evening, Raju," Vijay greeted, his smile broad and inscrutable, a mask of delight hiding unknown depths. "Enjoyed your day?"

"We did," Henry replied, his voice edged with nerves.

228

Vijay asked no further questions, yet his eyes caught the fire in Raju's demeanor. "Raju, what's going on? You're radiant."

"Nothing," Raju lied smoothly. "Just a sense that something wonderful is about to happen."

"Is that so?" Vijay's tone was light, untroubled. "You all seem weary. Let's dine."

They got freshed up and gathered around a circular table groaning under a feast of Egyptian, Indian, and Chinese delicacies. Vijay sat beside Raju, Alexa across from them, with Henry and Emma flanking her. Henry's eyes widened at the array.

"Uncle Vijay," he ventured, "something special tonight?"

"Not tonight—tomorrow," Vijay teased, his grin a crescent of mystery.

"What's tomorrow?"

"Wait and see," Vijay replied, his eagerness a quiet flame. "Eat now."

Raju held his silence, unsettled by Vijay's cryptic cheer. Alexa's subtle nod met his gaze, a silent pact to keep Vijay's focus elsewhere. They both ate sparingly, the abundance untouched by their restraint.

"Raju, Alexa, take more!" Vijay urged. "This is for you!"

"No need to worry," Alexa said with a breezy smile. "Henry's here to conquer it all."

Vijay's laughter boomed. "Well said!"

Henry flushed, his glare sharp, but Emma's gentle touch on his leg steadied him.

"Hello, everyone," John greeted them elatedly, striding in and settling beside Raju. "How was the museum?"

"Marvelous," Alexa replied. "We missed the Kings' Valley, though."

"Mhm?" John gave a brisk nod.

Dinner concluded, and Raju and Alexa slipped upstairs with haste.

"Raju, hold on!" Henry called, trailing them with Emma. They converged in Raju's room, the air thick with tension.

"I've figured it, Raju—stay calm," Alexa said, her voice a lifeline. "We wait."

"Be careful," Raju warned, his tone low and firm. "Dad said this is how we'll unmask the sword's thief."

"How?" Henry's question hung heavy.

"Their attempts to take my life, tells everything," Raju said, his words shadowed with certainty.

"You suspect Vijay?" Emma's voice quivered.

"Yes," Raju confirmed, unflinching.

"How do we know the sword's here?" Henry pressed, doubt creasing his brow.

"We need proof," Raju said. "Trust no one without a witness."

"Alright," Henry sighed, collapsing onto the bed, his mind a storm. "We're screwed."

"Don't wade too far in, Henry," Raju said gently. "This may be new to you, but not to me."

"How so, Raju?" Emma's urgency pierced the quiet. "These threats only started in London."

"True," Raju admitted. "I was caged for twelve years in a place I couldn't name, for reasons I couldn't fathom. I reached London after a strange turn. There's a thread connecting it all."

"Tell us," Emma urged, her eyes locked on his. "What came before?"

Raju's voice softened, a river of memory flowing free. "A bird in a golden cage, however splendid, pines for the sky. I lived that—severed from my partner, my son, my kin since the war. Only then did I taste freedom's worth and love's truth." Emma watched his solemn features; Henry and Alexa drank in his words. "Picture Vivékadeva, bound in that idol for millennia, parted from his beloved."

"I understand," Emma said. "But what is love, truly? How does it weave with freedom?"

"Love springs from 'Loobha'—greed—in Sanskrit," Raju explained, his voice a steady current. "To cherish one can mean to shun others. Freedom and love are entwined. Grasp freedom, and you become love; possess love, and you bestow freedom. It's trust."

Henry and Emma nodded, the revelation settling like dust after a storm.

"I trusted," Raju said, his tone darkening, "and they betrayed me—us all."

"Yes," Emma murmured, her voice tight. "What a cruel move."

"No, Emma," Raju corrected, his gentleness a quiet force. "We should treat the good and bad, happiness and sorrow, victory and the defeat alike, engage yourself in the battle! Thus, no sin will be incurred and no good will be pursued. It's the quality of a perfect man."

"Stability," Alexa offered.

"Precisely," Raju agreed. "We must embody it now."

"Yogi's on the wrong side," Alexa said, her voice sharp with conviction. "How can he claim the capstone's power?"

"He can," Raju replied, unflinching. "He serves his kin with unwavering faith, following their will. He's a meditator of rare skill."

"Even in wrongdoing?" Emma interjected, her words a spark.

"Perhaps," Raju said, turning to her. "He's unshaken, fulfilling his role—good or not, he stands firm. That's a Karma Yogi."

"Karma Yogi?" Emma echoed, her confusion a soft shadow.

"Every deed is karma," Raju clarified, his voice a calm tide. "A misstep breeds sin, trailing sorrow. But a mind in balance heeds no outcome—good or bad—and remains unbound. That's a Karma Yogi."

"So, the very Karma done by the common man is also done by the Karma Yogi" Said Emma quickly, "Am I correct?"

"That's true Emma!" Raju replied softly, "This citation suits to our Yogi!"

"What a cunning man Yogi," Henry muttered, his voice a low growl.

"No," Raju corrected. "The true cunning lies with the one guiding Yogi."

"Oh, God," Alexa breathed, her face paling as sweat traced her skin. "This isn't mere deceit—it's a kill joy of a relative."

"Enough," Raju said, his tone crisp and final. "We must rest. Sleep now—rise early tomorrow."

24

An assailant act

Before dawn broke over Cairo's quiet streets, a jumble of noises erupted from Raju's room. They all snapped awake, freshened up in a hurry, and stepped into the shadowy corridor. A sharp light glowed from a room down the way.

"See that?" Alexa said, nodding at the brightness. "Uncle Vijay's up."

"Thought he might be," Raju replied, keeping his voice low. "Let's move."

They edged closer, picking up gruff voices that grew clearer. "We've got to be there by noon," Vijay said, sounding rushed. They peeked in—Vijay sat in an armchair, four lads lined up beside him like soldiers.

"Morning, Raju," Vijay said, eyeing him, wondering why he'd shown up so early. "Oh, Alexa—you lot are awake too." He gave a lazy wave. "Come in." Raju, Henry, and Emma plonked down on a sofa facing him, while Alexa stood behind, leaning on the sofa near Henry.

"Today's a big one," Vijay said, looking at them with a steady gaze. "You up for it?"

"For what?" Raju asked, calm as you like.

"Giza," Vijay shot back, dead certain. "You know what's at stake, yeah?"

"To stop Yogi," Henry said, all wide-eyed.

"Hold up," Vijay said, cutting him off. He tipped his head at Simon, a lanky bloke next to him. "Bring it over."

Simon and two others lugged in a long, red wooden box—looked a bit like a coffin, with fancy flower carvings all over it. They set it down smack in the middle of the room.

"I know what's in there," Alexa whispered, gobsmacked.

"Open it," Vijay said, soft but firm.

Simon flipped the latch and lifted the lid slow. Inside was something long, wrapped in velvet. Vijay got up quick, stepped over, and pulled the cloth off. A flash of gold lit his face, and he looked proper chuffed. "This is it," he said, sounding grand.

"Vivékadeva's sword!" Emma blurted, jaw dropping. "Can't be real."

They all gawped at the ancient sword, struck dumb for a moment. But Raju stayed cool—he'd sussed out Vijay was the one behind all his grief.

"I'm backing Yogi," Vijay said, throwing Raju a hard stare. "He needs power. We're saving the world."

"How do we pitch in?" Henry asked, still innocent, though inside he was raging—You've done us over, Uncle Vijay.

"Not how you think," Vijay said sharpish. "Raju's got that spiritual knack."

"And?" Raju pressed.

"He'll take out Kesika with this," Vijay said quick. "World's sorted then."

"What about Pharaoh?" Raju asked.

"Dead," Vijay said, smirking nasty-like.

"Dead?" Alexa said, proper shocked.

"Plane went down yesterday," Vijay said, grinning like a git. He didn't know Pharaoh was still kicking in Giza, just heard about the grenade blast. "So Raju's my man for this. Yogi'll toss us some power after."

"Neat," Emma said, chuckling nervously. "That power brings Pharaoh back, can it?"

"For sure," Vijay said, softening a bit, clocking they didn't buy it. "Simon, chuck this in my car boot." He lobbed him the keys.

Simon and his mates hauled the box downstairs. Raju saw his shot and gave Henry a little nod. Henry tapped Emma to get ready. Alexa had nipped out while they chatted. Simon came back on his own, handing Vijay the keys.

Then Alexa strolled in with a tray of coffee cups and a mug. She dished them out, starting with Emma, ending with Vijay. As she poured his, she sloshed it on his hand. "Ow!" Vijay yelped, dropping the keys. Alexa nabbed them mid-air, spun round fast, and flung the tray at Simon's face. It smashed, slicing him up, and he hit the deck, howling.

Raju leapt at Vijay, smashing a fist into his chest, knocking him off the chair. Another lad came at him, but Raju booted him in the head, sending him crashing into the wall.

"Scarper!" Raju yelled. Alexa, Henry, and Emma were already out. He grabbed the room key off the switch by the door, flicked the lights off, bolted, and locked it shut.

"Stick with me!" he said. "Mind out—two blokes at the car!"

"They're nothing," Alexa said, cool as a cucumber. "We'll sort 'em."

They hit the car park and spotted Vijay's motor. Two fellas were hanging about. Raju and Alexa sneaked up, dodging between cars, while Henry and Emma hung back. Raju had a little knife ready; Alexa gripped a gun she'd pinched from Simon when Raju clobbered Vijay. They nodded and went for it.

Raju jumped the tall one, snapping his neck sharp. Alexa whacked the other on the noggin with the gun and bashed his face till he conked out.

"Done," she said, puffing.

"Jump in!" Raju shouted to Henry and Emma. "Giza, now!"

Raju took the wheel, Alexa up front, Henry and Emma in the back. He revved it up and shot off, tearing through the streets like a rocket.

"Good job we've got grub and water," Emma said, rooting through a bag.

"Fifteen miles southwest," Raju said, flooring it. "Hour tops."

"Yogi's crew'll be after us," Alexa said. "We need to hit the Great Pyramid quick."

"I reckoned Vijay was sound," Henry said, fuming. "Didn't believe you till I saw it."

"No worries, Henry," Alexa said. "We've got work to do. Where's the capstone?"

"With Pharaoh," Raju said.

"He's alive?" Henry asked, perking up.

"Yeah," Raju said, dead sure. "Capstone keepers don't die."

"Where's he at?" Alexa asked, keen.

"Round the pyramids," Raju said. "It pulls him where it wants. Dad hinted at that."

They were stunned by his odd answer but chuffed Pharaoh was okay. They got to the Nile's west bank and stopped at a checkpoint. Raju flashed a VIP pass.

"Related to the Antiquities boss," he told the guard. "Want more ID?"

"Nah, sir, off you go," the guard said.

They parked by the Sphinx and hopped out to find Pharaoh.

"I'll stay put," Alexa said lightly. "Can't walk."

"Come on," Raju said. "It's dodgy here."

"Personal stuff," she mumbled, uneasy. "Look for him."

"Fair enough—stay in the car with Henry."

"I'll stick with her," Henry said.

"Ta," Alexa said.

Raju and Emma wandered off. Alexa and Henry sat on the car bonnet, eyeing the Sphinx. The sun popped up, lighting the desert, and a dry breeze flicked Alexa's hair. The pyramids gleamed in her eyes.

"Henry," she said soft, "fancy a look in the boot?"

"Safe to touch the sword?"

"We won't grab the handle," she said, unlocking it with the key.

She lifted the lid and tugged the cloth off. The sword's gold caught the sun, shining on her face.

"This sword's done in greedy sods and good'uns," she said, staring. "Its power boosts you up but makes you kill anyone—mates or not."

"Crikey," Henry said.

"Master it, and you're strong," she said. "But no sneaky wants allowed."

"Sneaky wants?"

"Stuff you don't even know you fancy, like cash or clout," she said. "It takes you over then."

"Blimey," Henry said. "I don't want owt."

"Even Emma?" she teased.

"What's that about?" Henry said, narked. "It's love, not wanting."

"Oh," she chuckled. "Thought you were a nipper. You're well wise."

"We cocked up, mind," Henry said, serious. "Hooking Raju up with Vijay."

"Nah," she said. "It's alright. How else would Raju get his family back?"

"True," Henry said, gruff. "Raju and Pharaoh—top lads."

"We've got heaps to learn off 'em," she said. "To find the proper path."

"Yeah," Henry said. "We need 'em."

"Grab us some water," she said.

"Righto," he said, heading to the car.

"Oi, you," a rough voice growled behind her. She spun round—over fifteen hard-looking blokes stood there, a tall one stepping up—Iqbal. "Give us the sword."

"You prat," she snapped, whipping out the gun and aiming. They all pulled their weapons, pointing at her.

"Alexa, don't!" Henry yelled, too late as he came back.

She grabbed the sword's handle. A jolt ran through her, her face went red, eyes blazing blue. She lifted it, glaring at them, fuming.

Kill 'em, now, a voice roared in her head, taking charge. She forgot herself, all anger.

"Get her!" Iqbal shouted. His lot charged.

Alexa leapt up, flipping fast, and swung the sword, slashing two necks in one go. Henry watched, gobsmacked, from behind the car.

She hacked through 'em, blood splashing everywhere, dropping them like sacks. The rest legged it, but she chased. Three stayed back—Iqbal with 'em.

"Fire!" he yelled.

Bullets flew. She spun the sword quick, blocking 'em with a shiny shield. She ducked low, then shot up with a wild yell, arms wide. The shield blasted out, turning Iqbal and his mates to dust with a huge bang. Her shout echoed, hitting Raju far off. The sand went red, like a war zone.

"Alexa!" Henry said, stunned, stepping out. "You smashed 'em all? You've got it under control!"

But her face was blank, bloody and stiff.

"Sis," he said, "you need a scrub."

Kill him, the voice piped up again. She glared at him, cold and sharp.

Henry froze, scared stiff. "Oi, stop it! It's me—Henry!"

She marched at him, not hearing, sword up. She swung fast, but he ducked and ran.

She chased, swinging like crazy. "Leave off!" Henry shouted, legging it. She smashed stone pillars as they hit the riverbank.

He slowed, knackered. He tripped, got up, kept going. She caught up, sand kicking up under her. He fell again. She jumped high, bending back, sword ready to drop.

"NO!" Henry screamed, shaking, sand stuck to his sweaty face. He shut his eyes, braced for the blow...

25

Pharaoh's Wrath

Pharaoh rushed from the shadows like a sharp desert wind, catching Alexa. He jumped up, holding her tight midair while she stared at Henry. They crashed onto the sand, sliding and rolling over each other in a messy heap. Her sword slipped away, flipping a few yards before sticking half-in the dunes like a lost marker.

As soon as the blade left her hand, Alexa passed out. She flopped onto Pharaoh, limp. He got up quick, lifting her gently onto his lap. Raju and Emma ran over, looking at her still face.

"Thanks, Pharaoh," Henry said, calm but firm, eyes on him. "Is she okay?"

"She'll be all right," Pharaoh said easily, touching Alexa's forehead. "Emma, get me some water, please."

"Sure." Emma ran to the car and came back with a bottle. "Here."

Pharaoh took it, opened it, and wiped the blood off Alexa's face. Her eyes flickered, then opened slow, looking dazed.

A quiet scrape broke the silence—leather on metal. A man in black walked up to the sword, pulling it from the sand with gloves on, not touching the hilt. Henry turned at the sound.

"Yogi," he whispered, voice tight.

Pharaoh spun round. There was Yogi, smirking, with a hundred men lined up behind him like a dark wall.

"Well, isn't this nice," Yogi said, looking at Raju. "You're all here—and you, Raju, leading them. Worked out what I want yet?"

Raju nodded slow, staying steady. "It's not your fault, Yogi. You're just Vijay's puppet."

"True, he likes you more—kept you alive," Yogi said smooth. "But Vijay's the one who set this up. The BMW ad, your museum job, Cheops trouble, taking Alexa—it's all him."

"But you're the one caught in it," Raju said back, calm. "He's using you."

"A karma yogi doesn't worry about that," Yogi said loud. "Did you know Sunehri and I were at uni together—Pennsylvania? I really liked her, but I let her go to you. Fate split you up, though, and I won't lie—I enjoyed that."

Sunehri's name hit Raju hard, and he saw a nasty glint in Yogi's eyes. It clicked—she was with him.

"What's your plan now?" Raju asked, getting impatient.

"Tell your brother to give me the capstone," Yogi said, pointing sharp. "Then I'll let Sunehri go to you."

"Sunehri's not yours to trade," Raju said strong. "She can handle herself—she's mine, always."

"Don't get upset, Raju," Yogi said, backing off a bit. "I keep my word. Look over there." He pointed at a black car. A man opened the door, pulling out a tied-up Indian lad—about eighteen—then a woman stepped out, hands tied, still beautiful.

"Sunehri…" Raju said soft, eyes watering as he saw her. I've waited ages, he thought. Doubted everything— now you're here, like rain on dry ground.

Her face glowed when she saw him, the man she thought was gone. She couldn't speak, too overcome. Her blue eyes, dry from crying, got wet again. She looked at the lad next to her, then back at Raju.

He knew then. Vivék—his son, lost at five, back now at eighteen. The boy looked like Ishwar, the uncle who'd loved Raju as a kid. Is he mine, or am I him? Raju thought, stuck staring.

"I don't break promises," Yogi said, getting serious. "Get the capstone from your brother and come with me to the pyramid."

Raju blinked, focusing on Yogi.

"No," Pharaoh cut in sharp. "He's not coming with you anywhere."

"Quiet, Pharaoh," Yogi snapped. "Raju knows what to do."

"I'll go instead," Pharaoh said, stepping up, firm.

"And the capstone?" Yogi asked, unsure.

"You'll put it in the Crystal Chamber," Pharaoh said firmly.

"Fine," Yogi said, nodding. "Tie the rest up." He called to his men. "Leave Pharaoh free." They moved fast, roping Raju, Alexa, Sunehri, Vivék, and the others to a big obelisk, tight.

"Right, we've got this sorted," a deep voice said, steady. Vijay walked out, calm and in charge. "Stopping me for a bit isn't winning," he said, looking at Raju and Alexa. "I gave you plenty of chances, Raju. Saw you in the army, nearly told your parents. But Ramnath didn't like that—he wanted the sword back in the museum, no more capstone hunt."

Raju stared, ropes digging in, as Vijay went on.

"I wouldn't have it. Ramnath left after that, hardly spoke to me. I was worried he'd find out who you were, wreck my plans. So I paid the Colonel to hide your name, locked you up for 'treatment,' then got you to London—put you in the museum to use your skills. You turned it round on us. We even used your brother to finish you. It's over now."

"Don't talk about my brother like that, you tyrant," Pharaoh yelled, charging Vijay. He grabbed his collar and pushed him back hard.

"Enough, Pharaoh," Yogi warned. "Keep going, else they're dead."

"We must be quick, Yogi," Vijay said, looking at the pyramid. "Crystal Chamber—before noon."

"Be careful, Yogi," Sunehri said, voice tight. "Kesika might get you."

Yogi smirked, glancing at Vivék. Raju wondered— how'd she know about Kesika? Pharaoh and Yogi started for Cheops, everyone watching close. Yogi put the sword in a small pack; Pharaoh kept the capstone hidden.

"Original entrance," Pharaoh said, pointing at a dip above the fake gate's blocks. "It's safer."

"Right," Yogi said. "Let's go."

"We take the underground first," Pharaoh added. "Faster way to the chamber."

26

The hidden chamber

They hurried into the Pyramid and found a sloping tunnel going down. Yogi grabbed a torch from his backpack and turned it on. The floor got slippery and cold as they walked deeper. They reached an empty pool, once used to cool the Pyramid back when it was a busy communication centre long ago, now smelly from dampness.

"That's the way," Pharaoh said, pointing across the pool.

"You sure?" Yogi asked. "That tunnel doesn't look safe."

"Don't worry," Pharaoh said. "There're markings over there showing the way to the crystal chamber. Let's cross."

They moved slowly, holding onto the cracked ceiling, which was damaged from the Pyramid's weight.

"Oh no…" Yogi groaned, seeing the blocked tunnel ahead. "We'll have to clear it."

"Let's shift these rocks," Pharaoh said, starting to move them. "Help me?"

"Yeah, thanks for the help," Yogi said, joining in. "But hurry up."

They cleared it fast. The tunnel ahead was narrow, just big enough to crawl through. Pharaoh went first with the torch. After crawling for half an hour without stopping, they came to a big, round room with no air holes.

"What's this place?" Yogi muttered as they stepped in. Pharaoh shone the torch on the walls, showing old carvings.

"These will help us," Pharaoh said, getting closer. He pointed the light at one and read, "It's hidden in daylight, seen in the dark. It means the chamber's not easy to spot—you find it by feeling its energy."

"Energy of what?" Yogi asked.

"The door," Pharaoh said. "This place collected cosmic energy, so it's got a strong aura."

"You're a genius, Pharaoh," Yogi said, his voice echoing.

"Not now," Pharaoh replied, serious. "The door's here somewhere."

"Let's feel it with our hands," Yogi said, eager.

"Wait a bit," Pharaoh said.

"What's wrong?"

"There's a way to do this."

"I know it," Yogi said. "It's simple for us Kriya Yogis."

"Start with Tai Chi?" Pharaoh asked.

"Yeah."

They did Tai Chi for two minutes, moving into different poses, then breathed slowly—eighteen times, seven seconds in and out, holding for three seconds after. Then they sat quietly for fifteen minutes, calming their minds. After, they held their hands up and moved them around to feel their own energy.

Pharaoh felt a strong tingle, sensing something extra, staying focused. Yogi, though, kept thinking about the future—the chamber, the power—and lost track of the moment.

"Get up without touching your hands," Pharaoh said.

"Come on, let's look," Yogi said.

Pharaoh walked along the walls, hands close to them, while Yogi did the same, a bit rushed. Yogi went round twice but felt nothing. Pharaoh, taking his time, felt a warm spot on his hand. He kept it there, understanding it was his focus that found it—not like Yogi, who missed it, distracted, like someone ignoring water because of moss.

"Got it," Pharaoh said quietly. "This is the way in."

"Good job," Yogi said, annoyed. "Let's push it open."

They pushed hard on the hidden door until it opened, showing a passage like the grand gallery.

"What's this, Pharaoh? Not a chamber!" Yogi said, cross. "You tricking me?"

"Calm down," Pharaoh said, looking at Yogi's excited, angry face. "It's the last bit—no more blocks. Trust me."

Yogi nodded, unsure, and stepped into the ten-metre passage. Its pink walls shone, the smooth floor reflecting the torch, with bright, new-looking paintings. A soft gold light glowed from the end. Yogi ran towards it, too excited to wait, then slipped and slid forward. His torch rolled ahead, lighting a wall ahead. He got up and saw he was in a place unknown.

"We did it, Pharaoh!" he shouted, thrilled. "This is what I wanted!"

The pyramid-shaped room glowed a bit, like moonlight from the walls.

"Where's that light from?" Pharaoh said to himself.

"Maybe moon rocks," Yogi said. "They glow at night from sunlight, but there's no sun here."

"Could be cosmic energy," Pharaoh said.

Yogi looked up. "We need to put the capstone up when the sun's high."

"Where?"

"It's like the real Pyramid," Yogi said. "The King's chamber, where the energy's strongest, is at one-third height from the floor."

"We'll find it easily," Pharaoh said. "The capstone will show us."

"Give it to me," Yogi said, greedy. "I'll do it."

"Why risk people's lives, Yogi?" Pharaoh asked, steady. "It's not real—it won't last."

"It's for me," Yogi said. "It's not fake—not for Uncle Vijay or you."

"It's okay… There's a small instance to tell you… As long as there is a trace of egoism in me, I see God as the owner of the universe and all the beings in it." Pharaoh tried to enlighten him about the divine truth, not getting furious. "The Omnipotence and the immortality will only occur when you attain the fourth state, The *Eternal bliss.*"

"That takes too long, also there will be no importance of me," Yogi said, impatient. "Why wait for Eternal Bliss when we've got a shortcut?"

"Shortcut to what? Capstone power?" Pharaoh laughed softly. "You can't get it easily when I'm here…"

27

Facing destiny again

Yogi suddenly jumped at Pharaoh to seize the capstone, forcefully pushing him to the ground. Pharaoh kicked him back, sending Yogi crashing into the opposite wall. They fought furiously for a while. Then Yogi pulled his phone from his pocket.

"I'll send a message to my men to kill your family, if you refuse to give me the capstone," Yogi warned, showing him the draft message on the screen: KILL THEM ALL. "Just one click away…"

The sun was slowly rising above the apex of Cheops. Pharaoh reached into his trouser pocket and revealed the capstone. Yogi quickly grabbed it without delay. A trace of radiation began to pierce through the chamber's apex, intensifying rapidly.

"You should be ready to face danger when you wanna be powerful," Pharaoh said, calm and unshaken. "No phone signal works here."

Yogi hurriedly moved to the centre of the room to place the capstone. Using his clairvoyance, Pharaoh sped up alongside him. Yogi raised the capstone, gripping it tightly in his left hand under the radiation. Without notice, Pharaoh touched it too. Together, they placed the capstone beneath the cosmic radiation.

A huge flash of golden light burst forth with a banging sound, emitting a colossal vibration. The cosmic energy surged into Pharaoh's etheric body. The vibration flung both him and Yogi against the wall, then exploded out of the pyramid with tremendous force, scattering sand and pushing people away from the area. It travelled hundreds of miles at the speed of light, shattering all crystal-like materials—windowpanes, eyewear, and more.

Meanwhile, Vivékadeva's idol was being prepared for exhibition at the Cairo Museum. The director was set to announce its details before the afternoon, and tourists worldwide were eagerly awaiting their first look at this artefact. Museum staff busied themselves polishing the crystalline surface to make the silhouette inside more visible. Security guards near the idol peered at it, pondering its miraculous history, unaware of what was about to happen.

Suddenly, a thundering noise shook the building, shattering all the windowpanes. People around thought it was an earthquake and ran in all directions to save themselves. But two guards near the idol remained unfazed, not moving an inch. One of them turned abruptly towards the idol when he heard a cracking sound and noticed jerky movements in the silhouette.

Vivékadeva opened his eyes wide and smashed the crystalline wall around him into countless pieces, scattering them across the room as he stretched his massive arms, letting out a menacing roar that echoed loudly through the building. He leapt into the air and landed heavily on the floor. Standing nine feet tall, he had long, dry hair with a lock over the crown, no facial hair, pale-grey skin, and was completely naked, though covered in golden ornaments across his body. He wore crook-shaped armlets, heavy earrings, an emerald necklace, and a waist belt that reached down to his calves. His body showed no metabolic change since being encased in the crystal, preserved by his mastery of Kaayakalpa.

"Ooooh my god," the security guard yelled in fear, staring at Vivékadeva's enormous form. "Everybody run!"

Vivékadeva glanced around sharply, as if searching for something, then stopped at the southwest window. His crystal-clear vision zoomed in that direction, cutting through obstacles until it reached the Great Pyramid, where he observed the situation. Though confined for years, he had known everything happening in the world through his extrasensory perception and had visited many places via astral travel.

He recalled the memories of Vishnusamhita and the man responsible for her death. Sensing Kesika's presence near Cheops, he knew it was time to kill him. He swiftly leapt from the museum building into the crowd below. They scattered in fright within seconds, but media photographers seized the moment, clicking their cameras repeatedly to capture the rare sight.

Determined in his mission, he began to run swiftly towards his destination, ignoring all barriers like hills, trees, and water bodies.

Pharaoh and Yogi got up slowly, feeling no pain or illness—they were even more active. Pharaoh's eyes glowed with delight as he experienced a state of illumination, eternal bliss, and nothingness.

But Yogi seemed to be in a state of confusion, unable to realise what had happened to him after deserving the power. He slowly grew aggressive and lost control over himself.

Pharaoh understood what it was: Yogi had deserved nothing from the capstone except Kesika.

Kesika had taken over Yogi's inner aura and gained control. Tightening his fists, Yogi leapt furiously at Pharaoh, pushing him against the wall. They plunged out of the pyramid, turning transparent without breaking the chamber wall.

They fell with great speed, rolling over the granite blocks. The people around watched, mystified.

"There he is," said Alexa, pointing at Pharaoh. "He also deserved the energy."

Pharaoh punched Yogi in the chest; he flew a few feet and crashed into a stone pillar. But Yogi quickly grabbed a sword and began to attack. He swung sharply, and Pharaoh leapt backwards to escape it. Then he lashed out at Yogi from a distance. Both ran swiftly at each other, collided strongly, and tumbled over the ground.

"I don't want anyone powerful equal to me in the Universe," Yogi shouted furiously. "Get out of my way you bloody human."

"Oh…Yogi," Vijay expressed an odd feeling. "This is impossible, Yogi is under the possession of Kesika."

The atmosphere in the area began to change. A cluster of dark clouds covered the bright afternoon sky with thundering noises. Sunrays fell solely on Cheops through a small gap in the clouds, making it shine as if new. The sand around the pyramid complex started to shift backwards from the plateau.

"Mr. Vijay," Raju called him. "I wanna tell you one thing."

"C'mon, you've the chance," he replied, grinning.

"You both only knew how to use people. But, we only familiar with making people as friends, that is the same thing Pharaoh did."

"Did what?"

"What a fool you are? Can't you understand this after all?" Raju asked satirically. "Remember, Pharaoh is a best friend of Yogi previously…So, some of his men may also close to Pharaoh…Am I correct?"

Chaos stirred in Vijay's mind. He looked tensely at his men. "Stop talking like a saint," he cried lividly at Raju. "You also a murderer, killed many in the battle."

"I fought for my country, as a soldier. So, pain and pleasure is equal to me. But, you killed the innocents for your personal benefits," Raju replied firmly. "Now I'm going to fight for the world, as a human."

A loud crack emerged from the area where the Sphinx stood. Vijay turned towards it, unable to believe his eyes—there was no statue!

"Where does it go?" he mumbled, then shouted, "Not too late guys…Kill all these folks."

The armed men around pointed their guns at Vijay. He grew nervous and gazed anxiously at Raju.

"They're all police officers," said Raju firmly. "I already told you, Pharaoh did the same thing that you and Yogi done."

Twenty-five well-trained cops had previously infiltrated Yogi's gang without Vijay's knowledge. They were capable of stopping the remaining seventy-five. Confusion spread among the team as they tried to identify the police, and they opened fire on each other.

"GROOOO." A sudden roar echoed from the sky.

They all looked up to see what it was. A tiny shape resembling a lion grew larger—it was the gigantic statue of the Sphinx, come alive to protect the pyramid complex. They raised their machine guns and started shooting in that direction. The statue landed heavily, smashing the ground and killing some of the thugs by pressing them under its rocky paws.

One police officer approached Raju and unbound them all. Raju quickly stood and hurried towards Cheops. Four thugs tried to block his path, but he knocked them out swiftly. Alexa, Henry, Emma, Sunehri, and Vivék followed, moving stealthily behind massive pillars along the way. Suddenly, the Great Sphinx sprinted ahead, dashing into a pillar and leaping forward.

"Alexa," Raju shouted, pulling her back from the spot. Her hair flew back, covering her face, as the pillar smashed into pieces, raising a cloud of limestone dust.

"Careful," said Raju hastily. "I've to reach the crystal chamber immediately…Alexa, I need your help."

"What?"

"Stay with them until my return," Raju replied and hurried into the pyramid. Vijay tried to stop him by stepping in his path, but Raju kicked him aside and continued on.

Pharaoh and Yogi were still fighting each other. Yogi took a slight advantage, using the sword to deliver lethal blows and casting deadly spells. Suddenly, the Great Sphinx jumped directly at Yogi. He created a semicircular protective shield with the sword in front of him. The statue crashed into it and was thrown back against the pyramid. Then Yogi injured Pharaoh in several places and bumped him strongly onto a granite block, breaking it into pieces immediately. Pharaoh became unconscious.

Yogi jumped up, raising the sword to cut Pharaoh's head. Vivékadeva arrived swiftly at that moment, flipped into the air, obstructed him by gripping his arms, and cudgeled him against the ground.

Pharaoh stood wordless, watching this mystical event, and thought to save Yogi. Yogi had no power—Kesika occupied his inner aura. If any harm came to him, it wouldn't affect Kesika, and Yogi would be the victim. Kesika was in a formless state, called Akaasha tatvam, which was strong but inactive, immune to any weapon or element.

But the situation reversed—they fought fiercely. Yogi plunged at Vivékadeva and made him slide over the ground. Then Vivékadeva punched him firmly and kicked him into the air. Yogi flew a few feet high and dashed onto the floor.

Raju had already reached the circular room, following instructions from Alexa, who had been there before via astral travel. He tried to find the crystal chamber, turning around to locate the entrance. Fortunately, the door was still open. He quickly dashed inside.

Vivékadeva then took the sword from Yogi by force and throbbed him against one of the granite blocks at the pyramid's foot. Yogi got up promptly and flung himself at Vivékadeva. But Vivékadeva was ready to kill him with the sword. Raju spotted the capstone's location, jumped on it immediately, and removed it from the inflow of cosmic radiation. As Vivékadeva waved his sword at Yogi, Pharaoh hurried towards him suddenly and pushed him backwards very hard.

Kesika was disturbed and lost his grip over Yogi's inner aura due to the sudden removal of the capstone. He thought to form the silver cord with his body by directing him to the sword. But he was projected outwards with that sudden jerk in Yogi's body. He separated from him, like an astral body detaching from a sleeping person, with its glittering silver cord connected from the navel region to the same point on him.

Vivékadeva immediately slashed Kesika's silver cord with a powerful blow, fully separating him from this world. It released a burst of illumination with an enormous bang, brightening the surrounding area instantly. He not only took retaliation as the husband of Vishnusamhita but also saved the world from the hands of evil as a king. Pharaoh and Yogi rolled over the ground away from him. Yogi regained consciousness in the real world when Kesika left him.

The situation normalised—the Great Sphinx returned to its posture, the sky cleared, and the area filled with cosmic energy. Meanwhile, eight military helicopters arrived, dropping soldiers from four of them at the site while the remaining ones circled the pyramids for surveillance.

Pharaoh and Yogi stared astonishingly at Vivékadeva, stood up, and bowed to him.

"Thanks for saving us, my Great King," Pharaoh said happily. Raju emerged from the crystal chamber and saluted him by folding his hands. Vivékadeva turned to him and began speaking in Sanskrit.

"*Yadaa-yadaa hi dharmasya glaanir bhavati bhaaratha. Abhyutthaanam adharmasya tadaatmaanam srjaamyaham*," he said profoundly to Raju. (Whenever there is decay of dharma and rise of adharma, then I embody myself, O Bhaaratha.)

"You're the contemporary to Lord Krishna, my Excellency. So, you said it according to this juncture," Raju supposed obediently, understanding that those who kill evil become the personification of God. "Is that me, you've called as, Bhaaratha?"

"Yes," Vivékadeva responded in English. "From the word Bhaaratha, Bhaa means God, and ratha is the man who meditates; it totally signifies the man who interacts with God forever! You're an illuminated man, my son."

Raju felt blissful with that blessed reply. Vivékadeva gazed at Alexa and Sunehri and beckoned them forward. They approached timidly and took his blessing by touching his feet. He laid both palms on the crowns of their heads and called Pharaoh with a deep nod.

"You have a bright future my child, nice choice!" he said to Alexa, showing Pharaoh. Then he veered towards Sunehri. "You will not be separated anymore, live happily with your husband… Your son, Vivék, will become a superhero very soon!" He stepped forward to Vivék and fondled his forehead. "You should be proud of your parents!" he said to him. "You may face a great challenge in future to save the world and you must conquer yourself for that. Just remember: a genuine person will always change each and every danger which occurred to him as an art for living!"

Vivék nodded obediently and said, "I'm ready to face the destiny…"

"The best way is creating it!" Vivékadeva retorted.

28

The true enlightenment

At that moment, Vijay approached them, his mind reeling from the events. He was bitterly disappointed by Yogi's failure to claim the powers and seethed with rage at their loss.

"Vijay," a resonant voice called out. He halted and spun around in an instant.

He froze, stunned to see Vikram and Ramnath standing there, their presence steady and imposing.

"I've watched every step you've taken," Vikram said, his voice thick with anger. "You turned my son into a spiritual soul, yet you twisted him for something cruel—erasing me from his mind, ensuring he'd never seek me out, despite what he's become! You've spared me no harm, knowing I'm in London. Did you think I'm as good as dead? Is that why you dismissed me?"

Vijay's face locked into a blank mask, but inside, his steely heart began to smoulder.

"You've made countless errors to protect yourself—mistakes that can't be undone," Ramnath said, his tone firm as he tried to pierce Vijay's conscience. "Your elder sister won't even speak to you now, not if you carry on like this."

"You're trapped in a haze, clinging to a past you never fully lived," Vikram said, his words softer now, laced with a hope to reach him. "Find peace, Vijay. Stir the humanity within you. All that remains between us is friendship." He lingered on that word, his gaze piercing. "You're still my friend."

Vikram saw Vijay's eyes glisten, guilt shadowing his features. In a sudden rush, Vijay pulled him into a tight embrace, his grief spilling out.

"I don't deserve your forgiveness," Vijay murmured, the weight of his actions crashing down on him. At last, he felt a shift, embracing the present with a quiet calm. It was a transformed mind—what Jesus Christ had spoken of.

"Come on, Vikram, your son's over there," Vijay said, nodding towards Yogi, who stood serene, a little way from Raju's family. They started towards him.

Vivékadeva turned to Yogi, his voice warm and steady. "Don't let fleeting wants steal who you are. Still, I'm grateful for your part in this."

"How did I help you, Excellency?" Yogi asked, brow furrowing. "I unleashed that wizard—it's not aid, it's a disaster."

"It's no mistake at all," Vivékadeva replied calmly. "It had to happen for the world's sake. You let go of your pride when Kesika took hold of you." He paused, then added, "I destroyed him because he was a dark force. But who will root out the darkness in people's hearts?" His words hung in the air, stirring Yogi to ponder his true self. Vivékadeva stepped back slowly, drifting away from them, his eyes lifting to the sky.

Vivék taking the blessings from Vivékadeva
(A Pencil Drawing By Vis Dasari)

"My Excellency, please stay with us," Vivék pleaded, his voice growing faint as Vivékadeva moved further away. "Please, please, even just for a little while."

"There was no time to stay here, child. I must go," Vivékadeva replied softly, glancing back for a moment.

Suddenly, a burst of light flared around him, a shimmering blend of seven colours forming a balloon-like glow. He began drawing his life force upward, from the Muladhara to the Ajna. A thousand-petalled golden lotus bloomed from the Sahasrara at the crown of his head, radiating dazzling brightness.

His form started to dissolve, fading from his ankles upward into the golden lotus. Then, with a sharp bang, it vanished into the air, merging with the universal essence.

"Wow," Alexa murmured, awestruck. "What was that?"

"It was called Antardhaanam," Raju explained. "Vivékadeva has broken free from the cycle of birth and death."

After this, Ramnath, Vikram, and Vijay arrived, unaware of what had just happened.

"Yogi," Vikram called out. He faintly recognised his father's face, a memory from when he was four. "Come to me, son." Tears of joy welled in his eyes as he opened his arms.

Silence fell as Yogi approached. Words failed him, and he suddenly wrapped his father in a joyful embrace.

"You became good, that's all for me," Vikram said warmly.

"Yes, Dad, the whole tribute goes to Raju and Pharaoh," Yogi replied. "We should thank them."

Raju and Sunehri exchanged a look of deep contentment.

"I can't imagine the world without you," Sunehri said, her voice trembling with emotion. "I lived all these years with your memories. But there was a small hope… God wouldn't break my heart, and now you're here for us! I'm so happy." She smiled. "Our son, Vivék, will be even happier than me…"

"Yeah, Mum! You're right," Vivék said, stepping closer. "We'll be together forever."

They pulled each other into a tight hug, wrapped in a profound bliss Raju had never felt before. Nearby, Pharaoh and Alexa stood close, gazing into each other's eyes, their faces almost touching.

"What a happy family you have, Pharaoh," Alexa said, her voice bright with delight. "Will you share that happy moment for sometime with me?"

"Not sometime… Forever," Pharaoh answered, his smile warm and radiant.

***

That night, they arrived at Yogi's villa in London, except for Raju and his family. John was already there, waiting. He'd known about Vijay's actions and had quietly backed Pharaoh.

Vijay turned himself in to the police, handing over all the evidence of his crimes. He returned the sword and capstone to the British Museum. The court sentenced him to ten years in prison.

"Welcome, everyone!" John said, standing by the door. "Where is Raju and his family?"

"They've gone to India," Pharaoh replied. "He'll stay there for a month and come back here."

***

Raju, Sunehri, and Vivék landed in Delhi in the early hours. They took a black-and-yellow taxi ten miles west of Delhi, stopping at the house Raju had lived in before coming to London.

Sunehri gazed at the entrance with a wide, happy smile. Raju stepped forward and knocked gently on the door. No answer. He knocked again, then once more—still nothing.

Deciding to try harder, Raju raised his hand to bang on the door. Just then, the knob turned from inside.

"Why don't you knock the door little louder?" came a familiar voice.

"Mrs. Goswamy," Raju said as the door swung open, revealing her.

"How are you, Raju, my dear?" she asked, then gasped when she saw Sunehri and Vivék behind him. "Finally, you made it… Oh, thank God!"

"This is all thanks to your blessings, Maa," Raju said cheerfully.

"Come in… This is the day I was waiting for," she said warmly, ushering them inside. "Step in with your right foot first… Wait a moment." She hurried to the prayer room and returned with an *aarathi*—a lit camphor on a copper plate—and waved it in circles before them three times. She placed a dot of kumkum on Sunehri's forehead. Raju and Sunehri bent to touch her feet for blessings, and Vivék followed them.

"You should stay here, my children!" she said. Raju nodded with a broad, happy grin.

"Thanks for your help, Maa," Sunehri said gratefully. "For sending my husband to London."

"It's okay, dear… Everything will be fine… Come inside," she replied.

They stepped into the living room.

"Vijju," she called to her grandson. "Here is your childhood friend."

"Hi, Uncle Raju… Hey, Vivék, how are you, mate?" Vijju asked, walking over.

"I'm fine, but you became little bigger in size than I expected?" Vivék teased with a grin.

"Ha-ha-ha… It happens when we have an eagerness to see a best friend," Vijju shot back.

"Eagerness for what?"

"I'm just spending time thinking about you on eating."

"Hahaha," Vivék laughed. "You are so funny."

"Go and freshen up," Mrs. Goswamy said. "I'll get breakfast ready."

Few moments later, they gathered in the living room. Raju settled into a wooden armchair by a small table.

His phone rang...

"Hello," he answered.

"Brother, it's me… Pharaoh… See the newspaper immediately!" Pharaoh said urgently. "I'll call you back later!" He hung up.

Raju grabbed the newspaper from the table and scanned the front-page headlines.

"A SUPERNATURAL HAPPENING AT GIZA"

He shifted his gaze to another headline.

"RAJU: THE NEW GENERAL"

He couldn't believe his eyes and began reading the article...

Times of India, 8th January

Following yesterday's supernatural events at the Great Pyramid of Giza, the Government of India extends its congratulations to former Lt. Colonel Mr. Dharma Raju. Recognised as a war hero and a proud Indian for saving the world from the witnessed evil forces, the President of India has decided to honour him with the Veer Chakra and reinstate him into service as the General of The Indian Army.

Raju's heart swelled with joy after reading the piece. His dream had come true, and he felt a wave of triumph. Then, a quiet realisation settled in—something, or someone, had guided him to this success, the divine presence within every living being.

Raju, once an atheist now became a knower of the almighty; setting a perfect example for a life well lived.

"Vivék… A surprise for you," he said quickly.

*

Visually challenged boy pens novel

B.V.S. Bhaskar

RAJAHMUNDRY: Inspired by author J.K. Rowling's Harry Potter series, a visually challenged 18 year-old from a farmer's family in Gokavaram of East Godavari district, has spent seven years of his life writing *Pharaoh and the King*, a story based on Indian and Egyptian mythology.

Viswanath Venkat Dasari, a 2nd year student of the Rajiv Gandhi University of Knowledge Technologies, Nuziveedu, suffers from Nystagmus and Photophobia — his eyes cannot focus clearly on any object for more than a second.

Ever since Ms. Rowling's 5th edition of *Harry Potter and the Order of the Phoenix* hit the stores, Venkat began to weave a tale around the mythological stories he had heard during his childhood from his mother Satya, father Radhakrishna and grandfather, J. Harinath Babu.

As Telugu had been his medium of instruction, he took the help of his English teacher, K.V. Buchibapanna, and others, for proof-reading and corrections. He initially wrote by hand, and later, started using MAGIc, a screen-enlargement software, given to him by the L.V. Prasad Eye Institute in Hyderabad, and began keying the story of *Pharaoh and the King*.

The 276-page book, set in the backdrop of Delhi, London, Cairo and Giza, tells the story of a man who saves the world from evil. It takes the reader back in time to an ancient civilisation full of mystery, adventure, menace, righteousness, the supernatural and occult culture. The story revolves around a mystical being, Vivékadeva, who is set up against a villain who

Viswanath Venkat Dasari

robs ancient treasures from around the world and wants to misuse Cosmic energy drawn from the Pyramids.

The hero has been an atheist ever since he lost his beloved ones. But his experiences take him on the path of self-realisation. The bad guy tries to deceive the hero, giving him the hope that he can find his beloved ones if he will help him in his quest for spiritual riches. But, with the help of a younger brother, the villain is defied and Vivékadeva saves the world.

Venkat took help from his younger sister, Sija, in writing the script.

The book was published by AuthorHouse, U.K. Priced at $19.95, the book was released in the United States and the United Kingdom.

An Article on Vis Dasari in The Hindu Daily, 10th January, 2012.

www.ingramcontent.com/pod-product-compliance
Lightning Source LLC
Chambersburg PA
CBHW051150130726
47988CB00005B/2063